SORTING OUT BILLY

Jo Brand

WINDSOR
PARAGON

First published 2004
by
Headline
This Large Print edition published 2004
by
BBC Audiobooks Ltd
by arrangement with
Headline Book Publishing

ISBN 0 7540 7955 4   (Windsor Hardcover)
ISBN 0 7540 9700 5   (Paragon Softcover)

British Library Cataloguing in Publication Data available

Printed and bound in Great Britain by
Antony Rowe Ltd., Chippenham, Wiltshire

To Bernie, Maisie and Eliza

SORTING OUT BILLY

Sarah is besotted with the unpredictable Billy. But after another 'accident' involving his temper, Sarah's face and a night in A&E, Sarah's friends Martha and Flower decide that it's time to take action. What should they do?

- Reason with him?
- Send him to Anger Management classes?
- Hire a hit man?

Martha and Flower have issues of their own: Martha is seven months pregnant by one of three possible blokes: and hippy Flower's career as a stand-up comic is more sit-down and weep after some nasty encounters with south London's finest hecklers. Will Martha survive single-motherhood on a council estate in need of a peace-keeping force? Will Flower find the perfect put-down? And will they sort out Billy before he gets to them first . . . ?

My thanks to everyone who has helped me put together this novel . . . they know who they are. I am particularly grateful to my family for leaving me to get on with it and to my editor Martin Fletcher whose enthusiastic and friendly manner got far more out of me than any homicidal drama queen would have managed. Thanks to Vivienne for reading it all in one go and for making encouraging noises. Thanks to all the poor sods who had to drag through this, ferreting out inconsistencies and correcting my terrible punctuation. My progress from novel virgin to woman of limited experience wasn't nearly as painful as I might have imagined. Cheers.

Putting the world to right

Supplied by a cynical local pensioner!

Instead of giving billions of pounds to banks that will squander the money on lavish parties and unearned bonuses, why not put it into the *Patriotic Retirement Plan!*

This innovative pipedream revolves around the fact that there are about 10 million people over 50 in the UK work force, all of whom would be paid £1 million each severance for early retirement, but with the following stipulations:

Firstly, they MUST retire, buy a new British car and either buy a house or pay off their mortgage. The result: ten million job openings, so unemployment fixed; Ten million cars ordered, so British Car Industry fixed and the Housing Crisis repaired.

Secondly, they MUST send their kids to school/college/university and they MUST buy £100 WORTH of alcohol/tobacco a week. The result: the Crime rate fixed and there's the governments money back in duty/tax etc.,

It surely can't get any easier than that! However, if further funding is needed, have all members of parliament pay back their falsely claimed expenses and second home allowances! If this is thought to be unreasonable, then how about putting the pensioners in jail and the criminals in a nursing home? . . . . no, I'm deadly serious!!!!!

This way the pensioners would have supervised access to showers, hobbies and walks and would also receive unlimited free prescriptions, dental and medical treatment, wheel chairs etc., and they'd receive money instead of paying it out.

There would be constant video monitoring, so they could be helped instantly, if they fell, or needed assistance. Bedding would be washed twice a week, and all clothing would

be ironed and returned to them. A guard would check on them every 20 minutes and bring meals and snacks to their cell. They would have family visits in a suite built for that purpose and would have access to a library, weight room, spiritual counselling, pool and education. Simple clothing, shoes, slippers, PJ's and legal aid would be free, on request.

Private, secure rooms for all, with an outdoor exercise yard, with gardens and each senior could have a personal computer, television, radio and daily phone calls. There would also be a board of directors to hear about complaints, and the guards would have a strict code of conduct.

The criminals would get cold food, be left all alone and unsupervised. Lights off at 8pm, and showers once a week, live in a tiny room and pay £600 per week and have no hope of ever getting out.

Is it time for us grumpy old folk of Britain to speak up? . . . well, I think it is!!

M. J. HILLERY & SONS

Maintenance • Electrical• Plumbing & Heating

Family business serving Northamptonshire for over 25 years

WE HAVE EXPANDED OUR RANGE OF SERVICES TO INCLUDE:

CARPENTRY—KITCHEN FITTING
DECORATING—PLASTERING
FLOORING—TILING

IN ADDITION TO OUR EXISTING SERVICES:

GAS SAFE CERTIFICATION—LANDLORDS INSPECTIONS
BOILERS SERVICED AND INSTALLED
FULL HEATING SYSTEMS—COOKERS & FIRES INSTALLED
BATHROOMS & SHOWER ROOMS
ELECTRIC HEATING SYSTEMS—FULL REWIRES
EXTRA SOCKETS & LIGHTS—SECURITY ALARMS
SMOKE DETECTORS—CCTV SYSTEMS

INSURANCE APPROVED CONTRACTORS

CALL MARK ON 01604 411788
The only number you need

Registered through:
NICEIC

PROLOGUE

Martha could remember exactly when it was that she had first started hating her father. She was four years old. Before that, she had simply felt a sense of unease about the harshness of his voice, his unpleasantly smelling hands and the way her mother Pat spent most of the day looking like a rabbit that has been taken out of its cage by some schoolboys and is about to be tortured.

The Day of Hate should have been a very joyous occasion because it was her sister Mary's seventh birthday, and in an uncharacteristically generous gesture, the Rev Brian had decided to throw a party for her. He had asked some friends and family round, but very few of either group had responded to the offer because his family didn't like him and most of his friends were in the process of becoming unfriends.

As the Harris family so rarely entertained, the Rev Brian was in a state of advanced anxiety, manifested as a mixture of bad temper and mild hysteria. This worried Martha. Some children from Mary's class in the small Suffolk village school had been roped in—under duress as none of them, despite the fact that they quite liked Mary, actually wanted to spend any time in the house of 'Reverend Smelly Belly' because he scared them. His nasal hair had been allowed to get out of control and as he always spoke to people—even small children—by shoving his face only a few inches away from theirs, it was enough to make a seven year old cry. Besides, he was a vicar.

1

So Rev Brian did his best to be an entertaining host, but after a couple of hours, the strain of marshalling ten grubby village children in what he considered to be his beautiful home and seeing dirty fingers travel up and down the curtains, pictures and wallpaper, his thin veneer of amiability was beginning to slip away.

Mary copped it first during a game of Pass the Parcel when she screamed a little too delightedly for the Reverend Brian's fragile state. He hauled her into a room out of earshot and smacked her with the words, 'Keep-the-noise-down-you-silly-girl-and-don't-show-me-up.' Mary had no idea what this last bit meant and was so shocked she almost forgot to cry.

Pat Harris, oblivious to the changing moods of her sulky husband, was in the kitchen humming and putting candles on the cake when the Rev Brian stamped in and said he had had enough of the little shits ruining the place, and that he was going to entertain the marauding gang of plebs in the garden, where they couldn't do any damage.

'Oh, come on, Brian,' said Pat, 'it's only once in a blue moon and they're having such fun. It's nice to hear them laughing and see their little faces looking so happy. Please don't ruin it, dear.'

This was too much for the Reverend, who had been bubbling under since that little Jim Baker from the village had cried when he discovered that the prize for winning Pass the Parcel was a Bible and since Kim Meades had wet her pants over the Persian rug in the hall when he shouted at her. He finally blew a gasket and marched Pat, holding her by the ear, through the party room, announcing as he passed that one thing he couldn't abide was a cocky woman and the only way to deal with her was to discipline her.

Under the fixed gazes of Martha and Mary and to the confusion of the guests, he pushed Pat, who was desperately trying to make a joke out of the whole thing, into the cupboard under the stairs and locked it.

'And stay there until you've learned some manners,' he said.

Even at the age of four, Martha was mortified. Pat could be heard, pleading in her gentle voice to be let out, but Rev Brian wasn't having any of it. He led everyone out into the garden, dismissing any protests and proving once again that people will pretty much do what they are told as long as someone is enough of a bully.

Martha could not contain her anger, and marching up to her father with all the sophistication and language control a four year old could manage, gave it to him right between the eyes. 'I hate you, I hate you,' she said. 'You are a ...' she hesitated. 'You are a wanker, Dad.'

Time stood still as the Rev Brian bore down upon her like a musty avalanche, scooped her up and carried her into the house. He took Martha to the bathroom where he pushed a lump of soap into her mouth. Then he hung her out of the bathroom window in as jokey a way as he could manage and shouted, 'Here she is, we're only having a bit of fun!' His voice sounded as if his testicles had recently been removed and made the word 'fun' sound as if it meant murder.

This was too much for the ordinary village families, who filed out of the vicarage garden and as soon as they were out, quickened their pace, giggling and whispering, eager to tell whoever they could as fast as they could.

It was many months before the Rev Brian was given absolution by the village for his behaviour that day, and Mary, Pat and Martha were punished for all that period, as naturally it was *their fault*.

As time passed on, things didn't get any better between Martha and her dad because Martha had decided to fight him at every opportunity. Mary, on the other hand, had decided she would submit and that would make life a lot easier. It was. The Reverend pretty much ignored her from then on, apart from the occasional scathing comment about her looks, domestic competence or choice of husband.

Both Martha and Mary had to be confirmed despite the fact that Martha had chosen, at around the age of six, to be an atheist, because she felt if God existed He wouldn't ever allow the sort of behaviour the Rev indulged in. It was on this occasion that her father took the opportunity to give a little talk to the congregation about the nature of God, illustrating it with some stories from family life, the dénouement of which was the relating of an incident which had happened the week before.

'Now my daughter Martha is a difficult little cuss at the best of times,' said the Reverend Brian, 'and not only that, she is quite greedy. Last week, for example, my wife Pat made some homemade lemonade which Martha loves and despite us urging moderation she drank gallons of the stuff. Consequently that night she wet her bed—can you believe it of a girl of eight?'

The children in the congregation sniggered and

the parents looked embarrassed.

'I am only telling you this because my wife and I kept warning Martha not to have so much lemonade or there'd be an accident,' said the Reverend. 'Now we adults are a bit like Martha as far as God is concerned: we don't always heed His advice but He knows better.'

Martha felt as if all eyes were turned on her and wondered how she would survive school on Monday. Pat and Mary both burned with indignation and shame on her behalf, but neither would say anything, because Mary was now almost mute and Pat didn't want to wind the Rev up.

After that incident, despite the number of times Martha prayed desperately in the little church, she couldn't get God to admit that her dad was doing a crap PR job for Him or even give her a clue that He could see what she meant.

The Rev Brian haunted Martha's nightmares for the rest of her childhood and popped into her adult dreams with alarming frequency as well. He was tolerated by the villagers who all knew he was a bit of a bastard to his family but they found him good at his job, efficient and businesslike, and therefore were prepared to accept the slightly Dickensian attitude he took towards the three women in his life.

By the time she was a teenager, Martha's relationship with her father was constantly stirred to boiling point by the added ingredient of hormonal changes. Martha had thought the Rev Brian couldn't get any worse but then he showed a side to his nature she wasn't prepared for: he became a bit of a lech. After one evening when the Reverend, sweating and embarrassingly over-attentive, clingily waited hand and foot on Martha and her friend Joelle whose bosoms were enormous, Martha decided to size up friends on the basis of how much they would sexually arouse the Rev and hence a series of spotty, unattractive teenage girls could often be seen trudging in and out of the vicarage as if all beauty and animation had been banned. Boyfriends were recruited solely on the basis of their unsuitablility, Martha bussing in drug-users and working-class boys to wind up her father and becoming sexually active at the age of fourteen.

She lost her virginity to a local farmworker who was nineteen and she fantasised about a shotgun wedding ceremony conducted by her father, head in his cheesy hands.

Mary was neither help nor hindrance in the battle against the Reverend Brian and like a great sulking bat withdrew to her bedroom for most of her teenage years and surrounded herself with Gothic paraphernalia and dressed herself in the manner of a Victorian widow with a penchant for erotica.

Pat, who had been an innocent, cheerful farmer's daughter attracted by the brooding bad temper of Brian as a young man, constantly berated herself for allowing her husband to treat her two daughters as if they were dangerous dogs that needed to be taught who was boss.

And despite the fact that she knew her husband was a pathetic bully, she could not quite bring herself to administer the coup-de-grace of a divorce because she wanted to feel that underneath the sulking, bad-tempered surface there was an intellectual and an idealist who still loved her very

6

much. Unfortunately he had been replaced by this malodorous, labile old fart within a very short time of them having married, and it seemed unlikely that pre-marriage Brian would ever resurface. So Pat sat through many humiliations, both public and private, about which she was enormously ashamed and the little whispers she always seemed to hear behind her when she went to the village for some shopping or to borrow books from the library always seemed to say, 'Pat you are pathetic, Pat you are weak, Pat you deserve what you get.' Eventually she believed it.

The Reverend Brian did go through a period in Martha's twenties of temporarily being struck by the teaching of Christianity as a true force for good and he thought he'd better try and win back the respect of his daughters.

Mary wasn't too difficult. By that time she had married Derek the skull and anything which interrupted the tedium of their ordered life was welcome even if it was her irritable father attempting to slime his way back into her affections.

In contrast Martha stood firm and continued to notch up a series of coronary-inducing firsts for the Reverend Brian, including having a tattoo which said *Jesus Sucks* on her bum and flashing it on the odd occasion in the village when she was pissed, dropping out of college, becoming a Muslim for a while and getting a job as a waitress in a strip club in Soho.

Her three ambitions were to be a single mother, to see her mum happy, and to have her father on his knees begging for forgiveness. If he was naked and covered in the contents of a rubbish bin, all the better.

7

status quo, she, much more than the others, had been on a long-term pilgrimage to find a man to validate her existence in the starring role of husband and sperm provider for the future production of children. She had already worked out the kids' names (Nathan and Emily), what they would wear at their Christenings and she wanted an elective Caesarean because this involved fewer unpleasant fluids cascading over her nightie. (No one had told Sarah yet that in the birthing process, a pretty nightie tends to metamorphose into a butcher's apron.) Sarah found herself somewhat miffed when Martha announced her forthcoming event, in the pub, to her and Flower.

'Are you sure you're pregnant?' she said.

'Well, I've done a test,' said Martha.

'Oh, I'd do another one—they don't always work, you know,' said Sarah.

'Bollocks! Yes, they do,' said Martha, sensing something in Sarah's voice. 'Don't worry Sar. It is written that you will produce some little buggers. And Connie begat Sarah begat Nathan and Emily,' she announced in biblical tones to the pub, whilst Sarah looked nonplussed and wondered if her friend had gone bonkers.

*   *   *

The three always met at the same pub, the King's Head near the Oval cricket ground. It stood, Victorian, scarred and lonely, surrounded by 1950s estates, like the sole survivor of a bombing raid, and glowed at night like a dying ember amongst the harsher neon lights of a threatening, scarier age.

Martha set off for the pub at seven and was

13

pleased to see it was raining. She felt safer in the rain. She assumed that burglars and rapists didn't go out when it was raining because at heart, they were lazy, pathetic bastards who were reluctant to get wet.

Sarah was heading to the pub from a different direction. She hated the rain. It made her make-up run, her clothes look shite, and meant she turned up at places where potential husbands might be lurking looking bedraggled and unmarriageable. Martha, Flower and Sarah were all in their mid- to late-thirties and Sarah rather regretted the fact that she'd missed out on being a ladette because she was too old. Had she been able to run around drinking beer and swearing she thought that would have given her life so much more meaning.

Being six foot tall, the rain always hit Flower before everybody else and she would happily raise her head and let it run over the make-up-free zone that was her face. Sarah was appalled by Flower's refusal to wear make-up. To her it was like going without pants. Flower hadn't actually told Sarah she was knickerless too!

Although she didn't like to admit it because people thought she was a ballsy feminist, Martha was absolutely terrified of negotiating the rubbish-cluttered street round where she lived at night, because of the gangs of what would have been considered ten years ago, relatively young lads. Now, with the benefit of better diets, they were testosterone-soaked, huge, grown-up men in the bodies of fourteen year olds whose vocabulary of swearwords and sexist abuse was precisely targeted, if not vast. They could also smell fear, and its presence in their nostrils led them to track Martha

14

along the road, trying to make her cry. It didn't take much, given that her hormone content was running at about 97 per cent of her body mass, so even if someone shouted something as harmless as, 'Up the duff!' at her, she would be reduced to tears. And these were South London boys. They weren't going to stop at something as Ealing Comedy as 'Up the duff!' Oh no. Poor old Martha was regaled with everything their poor starved imaginations could come up with, and with her head down, she marched on wishing that the cane was still used in school and that capital punishment existed for the extra special crime of calling someone 'a fat slag'.

'Fuck off!' she retorted, wishing she didn't sound quite so much like a language coach from Surrey.

Flower, because of her height, her bicycle and her socialworkeresque appearance, also suffered the harsh verbal slings and arrows of the public, but it tended to be more amused banter than vitriolic abuse, until one day, a car full of lads had passed and one of them leaned out to pull her plait.

'Oi!' he shouted. 'It's a fucking giraffe on a bike!'

Flower had discovered in herself a rage she did not know she was capable of. She followed them to the next set of lights, pulled off their windscreen wipers and kicked the side of the car, oblivious to the fact that they could kill her if they wanted to. Lucky for her, they were more bemused than angry to see this angular girl lay into their car, and she escaped without injury.

Sarah, on the other hand, was the sort of person who got a bit miffed if some medieval sex offender on a building site *didn't* comment on her appearance.

15

The unlikely trio of friends had met some ten years before at a charity Christmas function aiming to feed and water London's homeless. Sarah had thought there might be some nice blokes there, Martha had thought there might be some horrible ones she could introduce to the Rev Brian, and Flower hadn't fancied Christmas dinner at home. They were the last of the single hold-outs as all their separate groups of friends gradually met people, got married and moved to somewhere with fewer asthma-inducing agents in the air.

The King's Head was its normal scruffy self, the sort of place where the last bloke to clean the ceiling had got nicotine poisoning. Martha liked its dingy corners, which hid her imperfections even in the daytime and, as she sat there nursing a mineral water and no fag, she speculated on the possible reasons for Sarah's phone call. Given Sarah and her foibles, it had occurred to Martha that it might be due to a bad decision in a shoe shop in Covent Garden at the weekend, or perhaps a haircut that made her look three weeks older than she was, but there had been something about the call that suggested otherwise. She looked up to see Flower, flushed and wet, heading towards her.

'Drink?' said Flower.

'No thanks,' said Martha. 'Just the one water always does me.'

Flower purchased some hideous concoction involving tomato juice, lime cordial and soda water, and sat down next to Martha.

'Well, what do you reckon?' she said.

'I expect it's something to do with Billy,' said Martha, who had only met the man a few times and had taken an instant dislike to him; even with

16

her limited knowledge of psychiatry, she had pronounced him to have a personality disorder.

'Multiple personality disorder?' Flower had enquired, having watched a film once about some woman in America who had loads of personalities.

'A "no personality" disorder from what I can see,' said Martha.

'Man-hater,' teased Flower, which caused Martha to launch into her usual speech about why being a feminist didn't mean you had to hate all men, accompanied by Flower slumping ever lower under the table with the whites of her eyes showing and a slight trail of dribble coming from the corner of her mouth, until Martha eventually noticed and shut up.

Then Sarah was blown in through the door looking almost human compared to her usual immaculate self. Sarah was one of those people who could wear a white suit in a coal mine and come out looking exactly as she did when she went in, as opposed to Martha, who seemed to attract flying lumps of curry onto her clothes wherever she went. Sarah, it seemed, had seriously let herself go, an indication that a huge crisis was occurring. To Martha and Flower's horror, she hadn't even put on any make-up, a disaster to rank in Sarah's book along with pet bereavement.

Flower had already got Sarah her bottle of fizzy lemon mixed with vodka and called something like 'Tropical Shag', a drink in Martha's opinion that was responsible for more teenage pregnancies and venereal diseases than anything else. Still, Martha couldn't talk. She, at the great age of thirty-seven, wasn't exactly setting a good example to local spinsters.

'So,' said Flower, 'what's the matter, Sarah?'

A tear began to make its way out of their friend's left eye and down her unmade-up cheek.

'It's Billy,' she said in a weary voice especially reserved for telling Flower and Martha that her latest relationship had failed in some oh-so-predictable way again.

'Has he finished with you, disappeared without trace, stolen your watch or sat on the cat when he was pissed?' enquired Martha, recalling Sarah's last four relationships and hoping to lift the gloom somewhat.

'He's hit me,' said Sarah.

Martha and Flower were stunned. Neither of them had expected this. True, they both treated poor Sarah's increasingly desperate search for a man and subsequent failure as a bit of a joke, but they hadn't prepared for this eventuality and there followed a very long pause.

Finally, at exactly the same time, Martha said, 'The bastard,' and Flower said, 'Are you all right?' Sarah responded to the question. 'Yes,' she said. 'I'm all right physically. He didn't hit me very hard, but I'm not all right up here.' She pointed to her head.

Flower, who unfortunately for her had done a bit of supply teaching and had had to wise up very quickly at a local comprehensive, not having realised that if fourteen-year-old boys were bored, they had wanking competitions in class, remembered a study she had read in which teenage boys said it was perfectly all right to hit girls if they nagged you and went into overdrive.

'Have you called the pigs?' she asked, an enquiry which because of its seventies' protest angle made

Martha laugh very inappropriately.

'Flower,' she said, 'you can't call them pigs any more. That's so . . . so . . . Greenham Common.'

Flower looked at her with irritation. 'I don't think now's the time to discuss my use of language,' she said and turned again to Sarah. 'Have you called . . . *them*?'

'God, no,' said Sarah. 'That would be well over the top.'

'What about Rape Crisis?' continued Flower.

'Flower,' said Martha, 'I'm all in favour of these organisations in their rightful role, but Rape Crisis—that would be bonkers!'

'What about a refuge of some sort?' said Flower, leading Sarah and Martha to believe she really had lost it big time.

'Shall we all calm down,' said Martha. 'Come on, Sar. Tell us what happened.'

'Well,' said Sarah, 'last night I was working late and when I got in about nine, Billy was watching telly and drinking beer, and he was in a really foul mood. When I asked him how he was, he just ignored me, so I asked him again and he told me to shut up.'

Had he been studying at the Academy of the Reverend Brian? Martha wondered.

Sarah continued, 'Well, I went into the kitchen to make some food and called out to him to see if he wanted any, at which point he came storming into the kitchen telling me to leave him alone, to shut the fuck up, hadn't he told me enough times already, was I a fucking moron . . .'

At this point she began to cry again, and Flower, who was nearest, put her arm round her, somewhat awkwardly it has to be said, for despite the fact that

19

Flower's mum and dad were good, old-school hippies, they'd been quite uncomfortable about the whole physical thing.

'So, then what happened?' said Martha who, subconsciously, had started to treat the incident as an omnibus version of a soap opera. Flower threw her a look which said, 'Can't you be more sensitive?' and Martha lowered her eyes demurely.

'I said to Billy, "I don't know what I've done, but I'm sorry",' said Sarah, 'and then he hit me round the face and walked out.'

'So what did you do then?' said Flower.

'Went to the toilet,' said Sarah, who was very regular and faithful in her reporting of the incident.

'And then?' said Flower.

'I watched telly, cried and went to bed,' replied Sarah. 'He came back in about midnight and—'

'Oh, I bet he was all over you, wasn't he,' interrupted Martha, 'saying how sorry he was, how he couldn't believe what he'd done, he'd never done it before, he'd never do it again, he loves you, he was so ashamed, he'd get help, he couldn't understand how it had happened . . .'

'Well, no,' said Sarah. 'He got into bed and went to sleep.'

'Yeh, but you're going to throw the wanker out today, aren't you?' said Martha.

Sarah's mobile rang. It was one of those ring tones you can buy from a magazine that is supposed to sound like a violent rap song, but in reality sounds like the tuneless musical accompaniment to some toy from the Early Learning Centre, so you find yourself humming 'Fuck the L.A.P.D' like a drama-school desperado on *Playbus* who hasn't moved onto grown-up stuff.

20

Martha could tell it was Billy calling, because poor old Sarah blushed and tried to sound businesslike and strict with him, when in fact Martha could tell that she desperately wanted to pretend the whole thing had never happened. After the call finished, Sarah, rather embarrassed, said, 'I've got to be going.'

Comments like 'Got to make his tea for him, have you?' or 'Does *he* need comforting, poor little bastard?' lay unsaid on Martha and Flower's lips, and they nodded semi-sympathetically. They'd both been there, not with violence, but with moody men who made them feel like pieces of shite, and felt that they should cover up to their friends and pretend they weren't that bad. Sarah was walking home now, wishing she had never mentioned 'the incident' to Martha and Flower. It would make life so much easier not being torn between Seemingly Proud Woman Who Doesn't Take Any Shit From Men In An Unacknowledged Yet Fundamentally Feminist Way and . . . Woman Who Loves Bloke So Much She Puts Up With Unspeakable Acts Of Abuse.

Martha and Flower sat morosely in the pub.

'She'll tell us if she wants some help, won't she?' said Flower. 'I get the feeling she doesn't want us to interfere. Maybe we should just keep an eye on things from a distance.'

Martha, who had been about to suggest they went round to Sarah's flat mob-handed, dragged Billy out, tortured him and left him for the crows to peck out his eyes, was somewhat taken aback.

'Do you want another of those weird drinks?' she said.

CHAPTER TWO

A week or so later, Martha emerged from the reeking lift and walked heavily towards her front door. Martha always felt relieved when she finally got into her flat after work. At the moment she was a waitress in a club in Soho, some twelve steps down the social ladder from the Geography teacher her dad had hoped she would be. Getting around was an assault course for Martha, not only because she was frightened, but because she was hypersensitive to the comments of everyone she passed on her way. It was more to do with the fear of abuse rather than the reality. The combination of the Rev Brian as a father, an overactive imagination, and a life spent watching rather too many films in which women got stabbed, burned, slashed, decapitated, strangled, garrotted, de-entrailed and generally not treated very respectfully, had given her an ultra-developed sense of vulnerability. She was the one at whom the presenter's reassuring comments were aimed at the end of crime programmes and on whom, like most other anxious people, they had absolutely no effect whatsoever.

Therefore, a knock at the door past seven o'clock at night in Martha's block didn't bode well. It was unlikely to be someone selling organic vegetables or a Jehovah's Witness, who risked crucifixion if they ventured onto the estate. Martha thought that the organic vegetable-seller would have stood up to the test of crucifixion much more steadfastly because they were healthy and full of stamina, whereas the poor old Jehovah's Witness wouldn't even have been able to have a blood transfusion.

But somehow the apologetic tap at the door wasn't menacing and although Martha put the chain across, she opened the door with some confidence.

It was a shock. Her mother, Pat, was standing there, having made it alive and proud through the middle of a South London estate with a terrible reputation. She, who couldn't even manage a night's sleep in the tiny Suffolk village without a light on and a cheese knife under the pillow. Somehow, this intrepid woman had made it past some scary, scary obstacles, not least the gang of McDonald's-fuelled, ill-educated hecklers.

'Mum,' Martha managed to say, with as little panic and surprise as possible in her voice. 'What are you doing here?'

'I've left your father,' said Pat, as triumphantly as a timid, sixty-one-year-old vicar's wife could manage, 'and I couldn't think of anywhere else to go.'

'What about Mary in Sevenoaks?' said Martha automatically, thinking less than fondly of her bad-tempered sister married to a shrunken, spotty collection of bones and skin minus a personality.

'Oh, Mary would just send me straight back,' said her mother, 'and she can't make a decent cup of tea.' (Vicars' wives' lives are punctuated with many very bad cups of tea.) 'By the way, what's an "effing minger"?'

'Never mind,' said Martha, touched that her mother still couldn't manage the 'F' word, and taking her very small case from her. 'Come in.'

23

She could sense Pat's fragile good spirits sliding out of her body as she came into the flat. Yes, it was grim. Yes, it was neglected, and thanks to a curry last night, yes it smelled. Martha didn't believe in covering up smells with commercially produced different smells. After all, there's nothing worse than going into a toilet impregnated with some entrail-shifting floral scent. Martha suddenly foresaw an evening, nay a week, full of horror, as she tried to entertain her poor mother while Pat made up her mind about her future. Martha almost found herself wishing that her mum had stayed with the Rev.

She knew, first of all, she would have to put up with a bout of spring cleaning in which her mother would do a passable impression of someone with St Vitus's Dance, accompanied by minute questioning of the validity of every single item in the bathroom cabinet, a thorough excavation of her washing basket, and a laundry session the like of which had not been seen since Flower's netball team all got diarrhoea after a night out at a local Italian and Flower brought their kit round because the washing machine in the squat had a sculpture of some pants in it.

'Sit down, Mum,' said Martha, 'and tell me what's happened.' Martha had an eye on the clock, because one of her favourite programmes was on in five minutes.

'Turn the television off, dear,' said her mother.

Martha turned the sound down, but continued to sneak a look at the screen, and when the titles of the programme came up and her mother had only got as far as the incident outside the bathroom this very morning, when the Rev Brian, according to

24

him, driven insane by her quiet incessant knocking, had appeared at the door, dignity dispensed with, various bits of himself flailing around, and landed a blow on her arm with a wet flannel, she found herself ever so slightly irritated.

'Oh, that's awful,' Martha said every few seconds while her mother continued the sorry tale, waltzing through what sounded like a comedy row conducted in every room of the house, before the dénouement in the garden with the woman next door threatening to call her husband and her mother's eventual flight from the vicarage with the vengeful words of the Rev Brian ringing in her ears. 'Don't come back here until you can stop behaving like a mouse!'

Martha had been at her mum and dad's a few weeks before to impart the news of her soon-to-be-visible illegitimate child, so her cushion-shaped tummy wasn't a surprise to her mother, but Pat Harris chose to tackle difficult situations by pretending they didn't exist, so she hadn't even mentioned it yet. Martha wasn't too bothered about this huge abyss in mother-daughter communication, because the sort of upbringing she'd had precluded mentioning periods without someone fainting. So, the two of them sat there for the evening talking politely like ladies at a church coffee morning, until Martha made up a bed for her mother with the cleanest-looking sheets she could find and heaved a sigh of relief as her mother disappeared for the night into the room she used as an office. It was only nine thirty. Martha still hadn't got over that teenage wonderment of people who can go to bed before midnight and consider it normal.

Sarah phoned at about ten, having got rid of Billy either in the bath or down the off-licence. It was a couple of weeks since the incident of the slap. Given the current crisis, it was of course impossible for Sarah to phone while he was in earshot in case she had to relate, second by nail-biting second, some recent incident between the two of them. Martha found her calmer and more back to her old self and under-exaggerating like a holiday rep.

'Yep,' said Sarah, 'I think I overreacted the other day. I mean, it wasn't really even a slap. It was a tap. Don't hold it against him, will you, Mart?'

'I'm not sure I could help it,' said Martha.

'Oh, please. For me?' There was a desperate girliness in Sarah's voice.

'I'll try,' said Martha, unconvincingly.

Martha wished she'd talked Sarah into ditching Billy and his flying fists, but instead she dialled Flower's number to compare notes.

'What do you reckon?' she asked Flower.

'Dunno, really,' said Flower, who was tired, irritable and not a little unsympathetic and temporarily floating outside her stereotype of a nice friendly hippy. There was the minutest of throat-clearings during a pause.

'Charlie!' said Flower. 'Get off the fucking extension.'

Charlie was Flower's bloke, a library assistant at the LSE who spent his spare time protesting about what an incredible mess the planet is in and how horrible most people are. Unfortunately, more by chance than design, because he was always in the thick of some sweaty, angry protest, he tended to meet quite a lot of horrible people, namely

26

policemen who wanted to take their frustratic out on his unwashed head and assorted anarchisı who saw every protest as an opportunity to rearrange a policeman's face into the shape of a piece of steak . . . unusual for vegetarians. Charlie, despite his laidback nature, was insanely jealous of Flower's every contact with the world and he attempted to monitor calls . . . as if Flower would phone her lover while Charlie was at home wandering about. Flower wanted to ask him who on earth would be interested in a six-foot-tall, vulture-nosed, failed stand-up comic and part-time social worker, but was aware that if he cottoned onto her sense of low self-esteem, he might bugger off too. One thing Flower had learned was that if you pretended you thought you were great and normal, nine times out of ten, people believed it. So that was what she tried to do. She often thought of Princess Diana and Marilyn Monroe and marvelled at how these women could hate themselves, although she knew intellectually that it was possible, despite the fact that Sarah maintained steadfastly that all the reports about low self-esteem were a mistake and someone who could shop like Diana couldn't possibly be unhappy in any way.

Another knock on the door startled Martha just as she was telling Flower about her day at work, and Flower agreed, as a safety measure, to stay on the phone while Martha went to the door, and then call the police if she didn't come back or heard blood-curdling screams. Martha herself knew that as the walls in the estate were fag-paper thin, any noises of violence would be heard, but ignored. In order to attract someone's attention, you had to

27

put on a record really loud, as that would bring the neighbours down on you like big, badly-dressed locusts.

Just before Martha put the receiver down on the table, Flower said she didn't think she could stand to hear her being murdered, as if it was almost certain to happen, and then Charlie chipped in and said he'd listen for her, and Flower screeched at him and an argument started. So as the knocking got louder and more insistent, Martha left them at it, thinking they wouldn't even notice if a twenty-minute excavation of her innards took place. She put the chain across the door and opened it.

The two-inch crack revealed a snarling Rev Brian with what looked like some dog poo on his face. Still, it made a change from the snuff that dribbled out of his nose and went unnoticed only by him.

'Is your mother here?' he shouted.

'No,' Martha experimented. This didn't wash, of course.

'Don't lie, Martha,' he said. 'I've been to Mary's, she wasn't there, and let's be honest, the silly cow hasn't got the gumption to go anywhere else.'

Martha wondered, as she had on numerous occasions, if men of the cloth were allowed to behave like this, and resolved to grass her father up with an impassioned speech at the General Synod. Something she'd read recently in the Sunday paper came back to her, a simplistic analysis of Freudian theory in one sentence, which proposed that men spend their lives trying to escape from their mother and women spend their lives trying to attract their father's attention.

Christ, how wrong can they be, she thought. She sensed someone behind her. It was her mum in her favourite dressing-gown.

'Pat,' said the Rev Brian, through the crack in the door. 'Come home with me at once.'

'I will not,' retorted Pat, quite defiantly Martha thought. But just as she turned to congratulate her mother on her stand, the words, 'Oh all right then,' sailed past her towards her father.

'Mum,' she said, as imploringly as she could without the Rev Brian cracking on that she was trying to take her mother's side.

'No, dear, I've made up my mind,' said her mother.

And five minutes later, she was dressed, with her travelling case packed. The Reverend Brian looked smug. Martha felt depressed.

Then Pat Harris walked out of the flat door, banged the Rev on the nose with a spoon, and went straight back in. It was a dessert spoon, Martha noticed. Perhaps the only piece of information she had retained from domestic science lessons.

The Rev Brian yelped, backed off and disappeared into the gloom. He walked towards his car with a thunderous expression which should have told the *Big Issue* seller on his way home to give him a wide berth, but no. A man with a dog collar was too hard to resist; at which point the seller felt and smelled a huge, slightly cheesy hand being pushed into his face and found himself sitting down in the gutter. So much for the Good Samaritan, he thought.

Arriving at his fifteen-year-old Rover, the Rev Brian found it daubed with words which, when witnessed the next morning in the village, gave

29

some of the residents quite a turn. The Rev Brian had presided over the parish for some thirty years now, although 'scared the shit out of it' might have been more accurate, and no one was surprised to see those sort of feelings expressed towards him.

Martha congratulated her mum and wondered whether she had found the little bottle of vodka she kept in her desk. Being a mother, Pat had naturally honed her ability to dig up drugs, sexual paraphernalia and booze. When she sobered up, things might be very different.

'We won't talk any more tonight,' said Martha. 'I'll see you tomorrow.'

Her mother padded off again. Martha cursorily flicked through the TV channels and, finding only the suicide-inducing crap that passed for late-night telly, flicked it off and sat thinking in the semi-darkness. She always left the big light off in her sitting room, as she only had lace curtains which became see-through at night and fuelled her fantasies about being watched by an army of self-abusing, frustrated old sex-offenders.

Gradually, she became aware of a tiny, yet angry noise, like a mosquito, and realised it was coming from the phone receiver. It was Flower, nearly hoarse with screaming. It was difficult to make out what she was trying to say, and Martha didn't need to bother because that very second, an over-ambitious, slightly hyped-up and very irritable rookie policeman kicked her door in.

CHAPTER THREE

Flower had always wanted to express herself artistically in some way, and being a grungy old hippy had originally intended to do juggling or stilt-walking, until it began to dawn on her how brain-fragmentingly dull it was and she had a vision of the future in which an audience tried to gnaw off its own toes while sitting through her routine.

In the end, she had plumped for stand-up comedy, her reckoning being that it involved the least amount of work for the most amount of money. She also thought it was crap that people considered stand-ups brave in some way. All right, so verbal humiliation from a sadistic member of the audience was always a possibility, but Flower thought there were far worse things. Her approach was pragmatic. She knew, given her height and general oddness, that she would be heckled by people in the audience and so she had attempted to anticipate every type of heckle she could possibly receive and have an answer ready for it. Unfortunately, this was not as easy as she had first thought. So, in her book of anticipatory put-downs, there ranged such possible replies as, 'Please don't be horrible to me, I've got a medical condition,' or, 'Why don't you fuck off,' both of which she knew she needed to improve on. The problem with humanity in all its glorious unpredictability, was that it kept coming up with heckles that she *couldn't* anticipate and which crumbled her comic resolve.

Flower was at the stage where she had maybe

ten unpaid five-minute slots under her belt and was trying to persuade a number of equally frustrated male comics, who had decided the only way they could make it in comedy was to run their own clubs, to give her a paid gig. Many of the problems she had were associated with Charlie sitting at the back of every gig and threatening to assault the heckler before Flower even had a chance to try out her put-down.

Flower had tried to redirect Charlie's energies in a more fruitful way by asking him to help her write put-downs, and there hadn't been an incident for some weeks now. An additional string to Flower's comedy bow was that she was a social worker. Social workers are desperately unpopular, because the decisions they make can never be tested, unlike doctors who, if someone dies, just get all their mates to say it wasn't their fault. Flower worked in a residential home for people with learning difficulties, although the children who lived in the street in which the home was situated still preferred to address them as 'mongs', assuming that this word shouted very loudly at the group when they walked down the street was extremely funny.

Flower had begun to hone her put-down technique on these little bastards without even realising it, and her latest sharp-tongued assault, she believed proudly, had left a twelve year old in tears. This was less to do with 'How would you like it if someone in your family had learning difficulties, tosser?' and more to do with Charlie's surreptitious clip round the ear as he walked past him.

Flower had received an irate phone call from

Martha after the police raid débâcle and had had to apologise several times in five minutes for calling in the Old Bill. She couldn't help herself, she explained, as the Rev Brian's voice sounded very frightening relayed down a phone line and when she heard his reaction to being hit on the nose by his wife, she decided to call the police, who were constantly on the alert as far as Martha's estate was concerned because there was often trouble there.

According to Martha, a group of hyped-up young policemen had destroyed her door and been pretty pissed off when they discovered there was only Martha and her mum inside. Martha had offered them a cup of tea, but taking in the state of her flat and Pat in a dressing-gown with the Ten Commandments printed on it, they withdrew swiftly, making a mental note that any trouble there in the future was likely to be a false alarm.

Coincidentally, earlier in the week, Flower had taken the liberty of contacting the police anonymously to find out what would happen if she called upon them in the future to sort out the Billy and Sarah situation.

Police operator: 'Yes?'

Flower: 'Um.'

Police operator (more impatiently and more unpleasantly than the first time, which had been quite unpleasant to start with): *'Yes?'*

Flower: 'I'm phoning for some advice.'

Police operator: 'About what?'

Flower: 'I'd like to speak to someone about domestic violence.'

Police operator (with a sigh): 'Hold on please,

caller.'

There is silence on the line—thankfully, thinks Flower. At least we've not got 'The Four Seasons' or something grim out of the charts. Just good old wholesome silence for a change. In fact, come to think of it, the police could show themselves to be the possessors of a good bit of irony if they played something along the lines of 'Fuck the Police'. Eventually, a gruff male voice con taining as much empathy as that of Travis Bickle came on the line and immediately wound up Flower by saying, 'Yeh?'

Flower: 'I've got a friend who's been hit by her boyfriend. Is there anything I can do?'

Gruff male voice: 'Does she want to press charges?'

Flower: 'No.'

Gruff male voice: 'No?'

Flower: 'Yes.'

Gruff male voice: 'Eh?'

Flower: 'Yes.'

Gruff male voice: 'Yes what?'

Flower: 'I can't remember.'

Gruff male voice: 'Call me when you can, love.'

Flower: 'Oh right. Thank you for your help.'

This last sentence was spoken into dead air, although of course Charlie was on the extension, but he couldn't say anything to Flower because he wasn't meant to be there. He wondered whether Flower was talking about herself. He tried to approach the topic several times after the call, but Flower's mind was elsewhere as she had a booking coming up. She was doing another five minutes at a small comedy club in East London which offered a

34

try-out night for all new acts and was known by the other more experienced comics on the circuit as Death Valley, because you couldn't make that audience laugh if you paid them. And so a succession of unsuspecting baby comics flayed themselves, totally unaware that they were pissing in the wind in front of an audience who wouldn't have been out of place at a gangland funeral.

That night, Martha, Sarah and Billy had come down to give Flower 'some support', although what support a girlfriend-beater who had a closer relationship with his computer than his girlfriend could give Flower it was difficult to say.

That night on the bill there were the normal no-hopers and budding comic geniuses who hadn't yet descended into the pondlife where they would naturally settle in five years' time.

On the bill was 'Muff Diva', a cheerful lesbian who mixed great opera arias with rants about castrating men:

'Evening, women and complete fucking arseholes . . .'

Then there was 'Edie Azzard', a female version of a certain very successful stand-up:

'Hi, hi! What would it be like if a horse could open a bank account . . .?'

And finally 'Dick Knob', whose comedy heroes included various sex-offenders and murderers. Dick Knob was quite a scary character whose friends had evaporated, given his propensity for trying out his act on them, since it involved a lot of spitting and occasional physical violence:

'I was holding this girl down on the floor earlier tonight . . .'

Five years later, an interested observer would

have found Muff Diva in a steady relationship with a male school-teacher in Sussex and working as a sports mistress; Edie Azzard married with three kids to the timpanist in an orchestra and going slightly insane at home while her husband toured the world; and Dick Knob presenting his own TV show in Australia and being fêted by his peers.

Flower was on third, and the audience was thin. Her supporters included a couple of girls from her netball team who never went out in the week and therefore were quite excited. There was a group of blokes who looked much worse than they were, as groups of blokes invariably do, a couple of friends who had wandered in looking for a drink, Muff Diva's mum and Edie Azzard's boyfriend, who was the only person in the world who had any faith in Edie's comedy.

Charlie was stalking round the back of the room waiting for someone to start on Flower as she stepped onto the stage. The smattering of applause she received wasn't encouraging and although the group of lads weren't child-killers, they had had a few bevvies and felt it was their duty to start on her.

'What's the weather like up there?' ventured the group wag, as Charlie pulled him backwards off his chair.

'Charlie, for Christ's sake!' shouted Flower. 'Leave him alone, will you.' She took advantage of the moment to launch into her longest speech ever.

'Lookatyouyoulooklikeabloodyrescuedogwhothehelldoyouthinkyouaretryingtoprotectmelikesomewankymedievalknightwithaweirdsenseofloyaltyletmestandonmyowntwofeetorwe'refinishedandstoplisteningtomycallsyouarseholeand . . .'

This was a bit of a departure from Flower's

36

normal material which was about recycling and the ozone layer, and the audience loved it because it seemed so 'real'. Charlie was taken aback by the applause and cheering which accompanied Flower's rant and, rather than taking in what she said, started to plan her new act.

In the dressing-room afterwards—well, not so much a dressing-room, more a small kitchen which smelled of rotting vegetables and dirty tights— Charlie went through a brief list with Flower. Then he went off to the toilet and as Flower, all alone for a moment, turned to walk out and rejoin her group of friends, she found her face about two inches away from Billy's, which had transformed itself from its normal resting expression of bad temper into snarling aggression with a side dish of spittle.

'Keep your very big nose out of mine and Sarah's business, you overgrown piece of hippy scum,' he snarled, 'or you'll regret it.'

Typically, the one time that Flower was really threatened, Charlie wasn't there.

'I don't know what you mean,' said Flower, sounding like Celia Johnson in *Brief Encounter*.

Billy sneered like a bad actor, but with some real menace thrown in. 'I know you've been thinking, you and that pregnant cow, of getting involved in what doesn't concern you, but just forget it, or there'll be a lot more violence.'

Suddenly his face broke into a warm smile. 'Hiya, Charlie mate,' he said, as Charlie came back into the room. 'Better find Sarah, get her home. She's got a long day tomorrow.'

He led Sarah away from the table as if she was five years old and Martha thought of suggesting he might like to get her some reins for those difficult times when his hands were full, but didn't.

Flower hadn't told Charlie about Sarah and Billy's bit of domestic so she didn't know how she could bring it up, considering it had moved onto a more serious level. And Charlie shouldn't have been listening in to her conversation, so he couldn't mention it to her. Flower grabbed Martha and took her aside.

'Billy just threatened me,' she said.

'Don't be ridiculous,' said Martha. 'Threatened you about what?'

'Well, I'm not really sure,' said Flower, whose reporting skills weren't terribly sharp. 'He said that we shouldn't poke our noses into his and Sarah's business, but how could he know? I haven't even told you yet!'

'Told me what?' said Martha.

'Well,' said Flower, 'I phoned the police recently, because I just wanted to know where Sarah stood if Billy decided to cut up even rougher than he has done already.'

'And?' said Martha.

'Well, they were totally unhelpful. I don't know what I expected, but since they've got rape suites and all that sort of thing I somehow hoped that I might get some nice, floaty woman who sounded like a therapist and would listen patiently to my problems then give me a considered and useful answer.'

'And you got the usual.'

'Exactly. But how could Billy have known I was doing that?'

'Lucky guess?' said Martha.

CHAPTER FOUR

Sarah and Billy had walked about half a mile towards the river before a cab went past and they managed to stop it. As they crossed Tower Bridge heading for Sarah's flat, the argument, which had flared up like a small fire in a wastepaper bin, had become a raging house-destroying inferno by the time they got home.

'Give us a fag,' said Billy.

'I haven't got any,' said Sarah. 'We'd better stop at the garage.'

'Why didn't you get any earlier?' said Billy. 'It's not like they're something we don't get very often.'

'I don't know. I'm sorry,' she said, but thought, Well, why didn't you get any, arsehole?

'Sorry's no good, is it? Can't you just remember in future?'

Sarah giggled nervously and her thoughts started to escape from her head. 'Perhaps you should remember,' she said.

'Oh, I'm *so* sorry,' said Billy. 'I didn't realise that I had to do all the fucking shopping as well as working all day.'

'I work all day too.'

'Oh, that's a proper job, sitting at a desk saying "Hello, can I help you?" like some stupid parrot all day long, is it?'

Sarah calculated that Billy had had eight pints, so it probably wasn't safe to push him any further. But she'd had six vodkas.

'Yeh, but you could make a bit more effort to do . . . stuff.' Her voice trailed off as she felt the almost palpable change in Billy's mood and knew she should have just kept quiet. Billy looked tight-lipped out of the window and Sarah wished:

She was anywhere else except in a cab with him.

She didn't love Billy.

She had done a karate course.

She still lived at home with her mum.

She had a gun.

Alcohol had never been invented.

She could be more like Martha.

She'd had her nails done today.

Billy could be more like Charlie and hit other people instead.

They stopped at the late-night garage to get cigarettes. Outside London, many garages stay open in the normal way all night, but Londoners are too criminal to be trusted with an actual open door; they have to use grilles like they do in New York. Tonight, every kind of person was queuing at the grille. Dope heads after Rizlas; young single mothers bored out of their skulls craving chocolate, having left their babies alone; a great big fat person who only ventured out at night and got enough of a hard time then from the group of clubbers buying water; and two boys on their way to burgle a house. Sarah joined the queue, while Billy sat like a thin, sulking Buddha in the cab. Normally, Sarah would have been too frightened to join this queue to hell, but given the mood Billy was in, she thought it might be safer.

The harassed Asian guy behind the counter was struggling under the weight of the single mother's chocolate demands, going backwards and forwards with each new request rather than taking the whole order. Consequently, the mob outside became restive like a post-office queue on pension day, and started to shuffle and grumble. One of the burglar boys happened to have a personality that was constantly at boiling point. Londoners are familiar with these characters and give them a wide berth. The queue parted for him as he sauntered up to the counter to purchase his bits and pieces. Sarah, two vodkas short of a challenge, kept her mouth shut, but desperately wanted to kick him up the arse. She was soon back in the cab.

'Did you get any chocolate?' said Billy.

'You didn't ask,' said Sarah.

'Oh, for fuck's sake. Do I have to actually bloody say everything I fucking want?' shouted Billy, as though non-verbal communication was perfectly natural between them.

The cab driver, who had been listening to all this thought, Poor cow. Why doesn't she find herself a decent fella? but didn't say anything. It was something he regretted, along with the many other missed interventions into lives whose inevitable progress he had left untouched, because that's what's expected. The most he could do when the cab pulled up was try and communicate his fatherly concern in a look, which unfortunately came across to Sarah as a slightly pervy leer and made her recoil.

Once inside the flat, what passed for Billy's public social niceties evaporated into thin air and his true face, the one only his mum had ever seen and which Sarah was getting to know rather too well these days, was revealed. Billy and Sarah had been together for two years now, and the protective veneer of romance which keeps bad behaviour at bay had long been scoured away. Normally this just

41

causes the odd row or ongoing irritability, but sadly, in Billy's case, it had opened a Pandora's box of flying demons.

Much of Billy's bad behaviour could be laid at the feet of his mother, who had brought him up to be a right little bastard. He was the only child of a couple in their thirties who had tried for many years to conceive and had eventually, to their disbelief, produced Billy. His mother wasn't a bad person, but she was a big softie who found it impossible to deny her son anything because she couldn't bear to see him upset. Billy's father tried to assert some authority but he had failed. By Billy's third birthday, a tantrum got him anything he wanted. Attempts by his father to intervene were rebuffed with such screaming that psychologists were consulted but their advice was rejected on the grounds that they were all weirdos who made perfectly normal children into miniature weirdos.

Billy didn't like women. Even his mother got on his nerves. A quarter of the children in this country have fathers who are not actually their real fathers, but unfortunately, Billy's dad could not even claim this privilege. Billy's mum had hardly ever had sex with him, let alone anyone else.

Billy's violence was unpredictable. Sarah had assumed that it would happen tonight but it didn't. He shouted at her a lot, called her a stupid cunt, and said her friends were a nightmare and she should find some decent people, although he wouldn't mind giving Martha one if she wasn't quite so bloated. Sarah listened to all this in a resigned fashion, knowing her response could either soothe or agitate Billy's troubled waters.

One of the problems that occurs when boy meets girl is that we are not called upon to give a truthful relationship CV to each other. Although our real personalities eventually will out, it can be some time before we have a sense of what our partner is holding back. The problems surrounding the history of a new partner are tackled in magazines for teenage girls and women under the heading 'previous partners'. Leaving aside a certain section of gay men who seem to have an inexhaustible appetite for sexual encounters, men don't want to hear they are not taking on a virgin, and women don't want to hear that they are. Apart from that, we explore very little of our partners' previous. Computer dating is a very good example of how utterly shallow we are in terms of matching people up and it is luck rather than judgement that puts the occasional fortuitous pair together. It doesn't actually matter a stuff that one person likes Country and Western and the other likes Easy Listening. Those sorts of differences can be ignored. But it does matter if one person is a bully and the other a winder-upper. If Winder-Upper is constantly niggling at Bully, Bully will explode and a pattern is set. The CV Billy never revealed to Sarah went something like this:

I never liked the opposite sex much, thinking they were a bit silly and stupid, but I liked having sex. I first hit a girl at school who was screeching and getting on my nerves. Her dad battered me to a pulp, which just made me more angry. My first serious girlfriend went off with another bloke, my second finished it when I pushed her and my third put up with

43

me hitting her for three years before she left. I like Sarah, but she's stupid like a lot of them, and if she steps out of line, I try to behave, but I can't help myself.

I was fairly bright at school; my parents sent me to a private one where I always felt like the poor relation and never invited anyone back to my inadequate home. I got friendly with a group of boys whose trademark was defiance and I didn't want to seem like a creep. So I failed most of my exams and ended up working in computers because it was not very demanding and I could sit back and do the minimum amount required. Also there weren't too many women around to get on my tits and I could have a laugh with the blokes there.

*   *   *

If Sarah ever kept a diary, she might have seen a pattern revealed of Billy's true nature, and could probably have worked out, with the use of a computer programme, when the optimum time to get out would have been.

24 January
Meets Billy in a pub when out with Flower and Martha. Chatting to him. Flower and Martha making 'He's a wanker' signs behind his head.

23 February
Bumps into Billy in same pub a month later. He'd been in there once in that time. Sarah had dragged either Martha or Flower in there a total of eleven

44

times. Billy asks for Sarah's phone number.

2 March

Billy phones Sarah and arranges to meet her. Sarah proudly points out to Flower and Martha that she hasn't sat by the phone all this time like a wimp but has led a 'normal' life. She doesn't tell them that when she is out she has diverted all calls from her land line to her mobile.

8 March

Billy and Sarah go out to the pub. He puts extra vodkas in her drink when he goes to the bar. She pours her drinks into a plant when he's at the bar because she knows if she gets pissed, she'll end up having sex with him.

She ends up having sex with him.

9 March to 10 September

Billy and Sarah conduct the initial stage of their relationship in a blur of happy feelings, laughing at daft things, playing games they will never play again, washing much more often and spraying themselves with a selection of chemicals, having uninhibited alcohol-fuelled sex a lot smattered with many orgasms and both Sarah's anxieties and Billy's grumpiness are kept at bay for many months.

10 September

Billy, irritable because he's had a bad day, is tired and has had a row with someone on the Tube, pushes Sarah out of the way when she tries to show him a picture in a magazine of a sofa they might buy. Sarah bursts into tears and Billy walks out of the flat.

14 December
Billy has been at the firm's Christmas party and comes home very drunk. He breaks two cups in the kitchen and kicks Sarah's cat by accident. When she remonstrates with him, he slaps her round the face with a wet tea towel. She cries because it hurts and he laughs because he is so drunk and it's a wet tea towel.

15 December
Billy cannot apologise enough; hung-over as hell he drags himself out to get flowers. Sarah is touched and forgives him. But when she tells him she has buggered up the video and taped *Morse* instead of a programme about the Jam, he tells her to shut the fuck up and leave him alone.

One spring day two years after they first met
Billy slaps Sarah harder than last time and she phones Martha and Flower. He isn't drunk.

*   *   *

Sarah crept round Billy for the night and things calmed down a bit. She was aware that in a breathy way, she was being a geisha, running round making him drinks and food, moving stuff nearer for him, finding the telly pages and keeping the peace. She could almost visualise herself in a basque, boop-boop-pe-doo-ing in and out of the room with a selection of tempting snacks and drinks. She kept quiet because she was in love with him in the psychotic sort of way that means you'll put up with almost anything, and as she lay in bed that night, she tried to work out what being in love with him actually meant in her case. Did it mean she couldn't envisage being with anyone else ever? No, it meant that he was nice *most of the time*, so that would have to bloody do. Martha had been sarcastic about her previous failed relationships— but were she and Flower laughing at her?

She woke up and realised Billy wasn't there. She put on an old T-shirt and went out into the hall. She could see him silhouetted against the window.

'What's the matter, Billy?'

CHAPTER FIVE

Martha to Flower 11.30 a.m.:

Martha: Have you spoken to Sarah today?
Flower: Yes, she sounded weird.
Martha: In what way?
Flower: Sort of stilted . . . a bit low.
Martha: It's probably that dungeon she works in
. . . they even have to write down when they go for a piss. They'll be measuring the volume next and setting a minimum level.
Flower: It's like when Charlie got arrested in Newbury. He had to piss in a pot in the cell.
Martha: Still, at least he had a pot to piss in. Sorry.
Flower: Call her tonight when she gets home. She's got a half-hour window before Bolshie Bollocks gets in.
Martha: Why can't you call her?

Flower: Netball practice.

Martha: Speak to you later. Hello, Charlie.

Flower: No, he's out . . . something in Suffolk coming up. They're meeting in the park. How's Lump?

Martha: Fine, moving about a lot.

Flower: Give Lump a kiss for me.

Martha: If I was that agile I'd get a job at the club blowing ping pong balls out of my . . . Bye.

Charlie to Flower 12.03 p.m.:

Charlie: Hello! Can you hear me? I'm on Dumbo's mobile. Are you all right? Some fucking bastard farmer's kicked me in the bollocks.

Flower: I can't hear you . . . love you . . . talk to you later.

Martha to Sarah:

Martha: It's me, are you all right?

Sarah: I don't know really, yes I'm fine.

Martha: Is Billy being all right?

Sarah: Martha, he's being absolutely fine, please don't worry. Please, let's just leave it . . . we're all right now.

Martha: Are you sure?

Sarah: Yes, really. I'd tell you if there was a problem.

Martha: All right. Are you OK for Thursday night down the King's Head?

Sarah: I don't know . . . I'll call you tomorrow, OK?

Martha: OK. Look after yourself, don't let him—

Sarah: Yeh, all right, bye.

Flower to Com Club 5.54 p.m.:

Flower: Hello, is that Martin?

Martin: Yeh.

Flower: I did your club recently and I just wondered whether you're going to give me a booking.

Martin: Which one were you?

Flower: Tall, hippy-ish I suppose . . . Oh hang on, I've got a call waiting.

Charlie: Who are you talking to?

Flower: Get off the phone, Charlie, I'm talking to someone about work. Hello? Martin? That was Tim from Jesters in Croydon offering me a twenty-minute spot.

Martin: Oh well, all right then. Twenty-sixth of April.

Flower: Thank you.

Flower to Jesters in Croydon:

Ansaphone: Hello, this is the ansaphone for Jesters', Croydon. There's no one here right now. Please leave your name, phone number and the number of tickets you require. This weekend's bill includes Dick Knob and Terry Hunter.

Flower: Hello, it's Flower Gardener here. I did your new act night, three weeks ago. Please, please can I have a gig, it's really important.

Billy to Ambulance Service 7.31 p.m.:

Billy: Can I have an ambulance, quick.
Operator: What's the problem?
Billy: My girlfriend's unconscious. She fell over, tripped . . . hit her head. Quick!
Operator: Address?
Billy: 17, Denbigh Mansions, Denbigh Road, SE17.
Operator: On its way.

Charge Nurse, A & E to Martha, 10.23 p.m.:

Charge Nurse: Hello, can I speak to Martha Harris please.
Martha: Speaking.
Charge Nurse: Hello, I'm Lesley Griffin, Charge Nurse at King's A and E. We've got a Sarah McBride here.
Martha: Oh Jesus, is she all right?
Charge Nurse: She'll be fine, just a bit concussed.
Martha: Concussed! Christ, what happened?
Charge Nurse: Well, we're not really sure . . . I think she fell down some stairs. She says can you ring work for her and . . . something about a flower.
Martha: Yes, that's our friend, I'll talk to her.
Charge Nurse: She doesn't want to worry her mum.
Martha: OK. Can I come in and see her?
Charge Nurse: Tomorrow.
Martha: Thanks, bye.

Martha to Flower 10.24 p.m.:

Charlie: Hello?

Martha: Hello, Charlie, it's Martha. Can I talk to
Flower?

Charlie: Hold on.

Flower: Hello?

Martha: It's me, Sarah's in hospital.

Flower: Oh God, what's happened to her?

Martha: Concussed, apparently. Fell down some
stairs.

Flower: Oh yeh? That's quite hard in a flat.
Billy?

Martha: I wouldn't be surprised, but there's
nothing we can do tonight.

Flower: Has she got her mobile? I might text
her.

Martha: That'd be nice . . . I'll go up in the
morning and see how things are.

Flower: How long's she been with Billy now?
About two years . . . I remember that with
Charlie, that was when he stopped following
me to work. Two years—that's when you're so
familiar with each other, you start to let things
slip a little on the mystery of romance front.

Martha: Hitting someone's hardly categorised as
letting the romance slip.

Flower: You know what I mean though.

Martha: 'Spose so, not that I'm the expert
recently.

Flower: How's Lump?

Martha: Lump's fine.

Flower: What are we going to do about this
Sarah and Billy situation? Do you think she
might give him the push now? I don't think it's

going to happen on its own. She's that kind of mad about him that she'll let him do this for years. I think we should help him.

*   *   *

Martha looked down at her pad on which she'd been doodling and surveyed her list.
Hang him and make it look like suicide.
Contract killing.
Push him in the river.
Tinker with the brakes on his car.
Giant kebab skewer.

Martha: I think we should encourage him to fuck off.

CHAPTER SIX

A faint whiff of urine, jumble-sale clothes and the sickly-sweet smell which clings to illness and death and has probably been commercially produced as a perfume by Joan Collins, greeted Martha as she entered the main door of the local general hospital. Being located in SE5 it found itself at the very centre of shabby scabbiness and witnessed a daily showing of stabbing, maiming and other acts of random violence. Martha felt like she'd smoked a whole packet of fags passing, as she did, through the collection of wraiths and strays that hang about outside hospitals wringing that final drag out of whatever's-on-offer-this-week-at-the-newsagents, before retiring back to the oncology ward to nurse their scalded lungs. However, their lungs hadn't been so shot that they couldn't manage a few cursory comments about Martha's appearance.

'Fat cow,' attempted a fat red-faced bloke. Martha had long ago given up on pointing out the fundamental inequity of this exchange from fat bloke to fat woman. The other smokers, including two women, cackled phlegmily. Martha's face burned and it annoyed her so much that after years of this sort of verbal public assessment, she still couldn't just let it wash over her. She was tempted to try, 'Well, at least I haven't got a terminal illness,' but that seemed way out of proportion. Instead she contented herself with a 'Go fuck yourselves,' at a volume not even a dog could hear, and walked on.

A sign on the wall pointed the way to a series of 'Wars', the Ds having been scratched off during a drunken rampage by some Casualty visitors who, not content with tormenting the staff in A and E, had done a quick tour of the hospital, pissing in the window boxes, writing 'knob' all over the walls and making the surprisingly astute observation that the founder of the hospital was 'a wanker'.

Graffiti of this nature always turned Martha into a rabid, big-bosomed Tory MP and she often imagined herself strangling those responsible with one hand whilst scrubbing with the other at the offending words with a huge Brillo pad. She believed that a decent environment begets decent behaviour—yet more evidence, Flower thought, of a lurking unreconstructed reactionary in her soul.

Ward 7, in which Sarah was stranded, was at the end of a long corridor peppered with soiled dressings, bits of fluff and the odd human blob lying groaning on a trolley. This scene would not have been out of place in Scutari, thought Martha as she and the Lump humped their way along, and suddenly her plans to eject the Lump in this very institution seemed mad and a home birth even in the dust repository she called home, seemed preferable.

One positive side to bad hospital care, she mused, is that at least it discourages the malingerers because one has to be really ill to want to stay. This technique, Martha thought, was also employed by teenage sales staff in the West End, who rely on people's desperation to buy because they always looked at her as if she'd just shat in their sandwiches whenever she made the first of many polite enquiries about whether they had any clothes that fitted people without an eating disorder.

Sarah's ward was a sort of grey colour, as were the people in it. The staple occupant of these wards, the elderly, allegedly confused woman, was much in evidence and amongst them Sarah looked like a child who has spent too long at her grandma's.

Sarah had two black eyes and some bruising round her neck. Apart from that, she looked great, thought Martha enviously, who in a similar position would look like a Balkan peasant who had not had access to 'facilities' for some years.

The woman in the next bed, who looked like Miss Havisham's mum, appeared to be blind and had been sat at the end of her bed for a better view of the ward for no apparent reason, was shouting continuously, 'Please kill me! Please kill me!'

'I fucking well will if she doesn't shut up,' said

Sarah grimly as Martha drew up a chair to the bed.

'What's the matter with her?' whispered Martha.

'You don't need to whisper,' said Sarah. 'She's deaf as well, you know.'

Martha started to cry.

'Your bloody hormones,' Sarah sighed. 'Come on, it takes more than this normally to set you off.'

'Sorry,' said Martha. 'Poor woman though.' She sensed Sarah wanted to talk about Sarah. 'So how did this happen?' she asked, feeling like a detective.

'Fell down the stairs outside the flat,' said Sarah, feeling like a suspect.

'Oh, come on,' said Martha.

'No, really, I swear,' said Sarah.

'Did Billy push you?'

'No.'

'Trip you?'

'No.'

'Swing you round by your hair several times until you had gathered enough momentum to clear the balcony, then let you fly?'

'No,' laughed Sarah. 'Look, it really was an accident.'

'I believe you,' said Martha. She didn't.

'Thanks,' said Sarah, who knew she didn't. 'Well, Bill and I had a bit of a set-to last night—no, no fisticuffs or anything like that—but we had a row and he stormed off. I assumed he'd gone out for fags so I went on to the landing to see if he was coming back and fell over a pile of new *Yellow Pages* some idiot had dumped there. I could have broken my fucking neck! Bill found me on his way back from the shop.'

Martha realised the woman in the bed opposite

55

was listening to every word and conspiratorially shaking her head to indicate she thought Sarah's story wasn't true either. Martha tried to summon up a look on her face which conveyed the message, 'Yes, I'm sure you're right,' but the look in fact just conveyed constipation.

'So,' she said to Sarah, 'how long are they keeping you in for?'

'Only tonight.'

'Do you want a lift home tomorrow?' asked Martha, even though she didn't have a car.

'No, it's all right, Bill will collect me,' said Sarah.

'Oh, that's good of him.' Martha was trying to sound genuine.

Sarah began gingerly to pull herself out of bed and reached for her handbag, a purchase which had cost her three hundred quid, but made her feel good as she swung it down Oxford Street on a Saturday morning while elderly people and weaker children were plunged by the never-ending bustle of shoppers into the path of oncoming vehicles.

As Sarah passed the end of the blind woman's bed, her swinging handbag caught the woman's head a glancing blow and set off another stream of entreaties. Sarah looked embarrassed, muttered sorry rather pointlessly and moved off quickly. Martha went over and held the woman's hands and patted them as if to try and convey she was sorry that she'd received a knock on the head.

'Who's that?' said the woman. 'Jack, is that you?' making Martha doubt Jack's positive qualities if his arrival was heralded by a bang on the head.

'That's her son,' said the woman opposite. 'Never bothers to come in and see her. She'd be better off dead, the poor cow, the way her family

56

treat her. We've often discussed bumping her off late at night, you know, when the volume of her shouting gets too much and the night staff just leave her to get on with it. Maybe we could get *her* boyfriend to do it,' she said with a wink, looking in the direction of Sarah's bed.

Martha rather liked the idea of a murderous coterie of seventy-year-old ladies in a medical ward, applying a spontaneous form of euthanasia.

'Anyway,' said another woman two beds up, 'what are you going to do about her bloke? You've got to teach 'im a lesson. We all think so, don't we, gels?'

South-East London's hardened elite of grey-haired working-class women was in an unforgiving mood and nodded its head as one.

Martha found herself slightly on the defensive, much to her surprise. 'He might not have done it, you know,' she said.

'Oh, pull the other one, love,' said a woman on Sarah's side who looked like a drag act. 'We saw the shifty-looking bastard last night. He done it all right.'

Were these women victims themselves? wondered Martha. She had a sudden vision of all their husbands as skinny little henpecked anorexics quivering against the wall protecting their testicles as these huge women ran riot round their kitchens. She tried to substitute it for a picture of bullying thugs but couldn't manage it.

Sarah appeared at the door of the ward having managed a quickie makeover in the toilets, bringing colour to her cheeks and sparkle to her eyes.

'Oh darling, you shouldn't have bothered just for

little old me,' said Martha.

'She didn't,' said a voice behind her and she turned round to see Billy smiling and holding what she considered to be a rather aggressive bunch of flowers. Why would you want to buy anyone red-hot pokers?

The eyes of Ward 7's women were immediately boring into him and urging him to do the decent thing, something unspeakable using a blender and his testicles, she thought. Martha half-expected pantomime booing to start or a pelting of Billy with used dressings and wondered why they hadn't warned her about Billy's presence with a timely 'Behind you!'

'Evening, ladies,' said Billy, and suddenly they turned from an elderly death squad to fluttery, girly girls.

'Evening,' they chorused, several semitones higher than five minutes ago and turned with great interest to their *Woman's Own*s.

Billy looked towards the shouting woman in the next bed who seemed to have slumped over backwards with her mouth open. 'Is she all right?' he said with such a lack of concern that he might have been looking at a friend's pet rabbit's eczema.

'Oh God,' said Sarah. 'Call a nurse.'

Before Martha could stop herself or even think about what she was saying, she turned to Sarah and said, 'You've killed her with your handbag,' and then she started to laugh.

The nursing staff arrived and drew the curtain round the bed affording poor Miss Lucas the only dignity she'd ever had in that place, but they could still be heard trying cursorily to revive her, not making much of an effort because of her age and

new skills you've acquired,' said Martha.

Some people, depending on how much of a personality disorder they have, are very good at lying and others are useless. Sarah fell into the useless category and therefore had to have the radio on and be turned towards the window when she told Billy of her plans for the evening so he couldn't hear her voice falter or see the reddened condition of her face.

'OK,' he said, not taking his eyes off the telly.

Sarah felt as if she was betraying him in some way and wanted to say, 'Look, I'm going to self-defence classes to learn some ways of dealing with you if you get arsey, because you have got a bit of a temper, not that I expect you to hit me again, but it's as well to be on the safe side because you wouldn't want to accidentally kill me and go to prison for life, would you?'

Instead she said, 'Shall I put the kettle on?'

*   *   *

Michael Randall, who ran the self-defence classes at the college in Vauxhall, was a genuinely decent bloke with two daughters in their early twenties, both of whom had been scared half to death by unlicensed minicab drivers at one time or another and had arrived home in a state of jelly-like paralysis and despair at not having been able to respond, despite the general 'bollock-kicking-I'm-up-for-anything-me' nature of the female zeitgeist.

Despite being a nice guy, Michael knew how the minds of not-so-nice guys worked and therefore knew that most men who assault or flash at women, rely on the victims being so terrified that very little

63

coercion is required. So all Michael wanted to do with his self-defence classes was teach these young women a few simple responses to get themselves out of trouble and allow them to get away. However, this would only have taken him twenty minutes, so he had to drag this twenty minutes out into a rather tedious seven-week course accompanied by more tedium in the form of aggression theory.

The huge disadvantage in life for Michael Randall was that he looked like a photofit for your local paedophile ringleader—sallow, wiry with thick glasses and greasy hair. Both his daughters were extraordinarily beautiful and if ever he and they were out together, people assumed he was stalking them.

The classes started at seven thirty and Martha, Flower and Sarah were in the pub by seven for a quick drink before what they all assumed would be karate-chopping dummies in the throat for two hours.

Flower, as usual, had been dropped off by Charlie who had temporarily acquired a van which smelled of dogs and cabbage, and she was dressed totally inappropriately for the weather, a cold, wet night perfect for a Jack the Ripper walking tour round Whitechapel. She wore a T-shirt, cardigan, jeans and flip-flops. Sarah looked like a minor turn-of-the-century Russian aristocrat on the outside and an American rapper underneath, and Martha who, because of her pregnancy was permanently boiling, wore a billowing diaphanous thing which was dark coloured, and some big, blokeish, boots.

The class was sparsely populated, a source of

disquiet for Michael Randall who every day looked through his local paper with growing despair as a catalogue of rapes, assaults and murders floated in front of his eyes. He knew canvassing for business wouldn't work: half the women would take one look at him and call the police.

Tonight eight women looked at him expectantly as he came into the gym which had been furnished with some of those rubber mats that are supposed to break your fall but don't. Martha, Flower and Sarah were the only new faces at the class and they introduced themselves to the other five, two teenage friends, someone writing a PhD on violence against women, a posh middle-aged woman who had been threatened at a cashpoint and a young Asian woman in her twenties who worked in a newsagents and had seen her father and brothers suffer the most appalling verbal and physical abuse.

'Right,' said Michael Randall, fixing his paternal gaze onto the trio of new arrivals, 'and what brings you here?'

Martha wanted to say, 'We want to know how we can all give her boyfriend a good kicking,' but instead said something very neutral, like, 'Well, the streets are so dangerous these days, we want to defend ourselves and our sisters.

'I realise that sounded totally wanky,' she whispered to the others.

It had not escaped Michael Randall's notice that Martha was heavily pregnant, Sarah looked like she had recently been battered and the third one appeared incapable of responding aggressively to anything.

He said kindly to Martha, 'Obviously you'll have

to take it easy with any of the physical stuff, dear.'

'Oh, don't worry about me,' said Martha. 'I'll make sure the Lump doesn't get in the way.'

'And you,' he said, turning to Sarah and trying a very sympathetic voice, 'have you been the victim of some appalling assault?'

'I fell down the stairs,' said Sarah flatly, knowing that the likelihood of that statement being believed in a women's self-defence class was about as likely as Billy plugging in and using the Hoover.

'Well, let's get on,' said Michael. 'Last week at the first session I talked about my daughters' bad experiences and we discussed some scenarios we'd like to deal with and this week perhaps we can come up with some possible situations and discuss how we might handle them.'

'How about a group of teenage boys calling you horrible names?' said Martha.

'What do you mean?' said Michael, looking puzzled.

'Well, fucking slag . . . lard arse . . .' said Martha.

Michael interrupted, 'No, I'm sorry, I meant what exactly is the self-defence issue in that scenario?'

Martha admitted that there wasn't one, but she would still like some advice on how to physically assault the offenders and get away unscathed herself.

All the other women empathised with this but were not surprised when Michael pointed out that it is an offence to assault someone who has not touched you and a rather foolish one at that if that someone is a group of ten teenage boys.

Flower then intervened with a story about a demonstration she had been on with Charlie and

make a list of the options for sorting Billy out.'

Martha grabbed an old envelope and put her hand under the settee where several pens lay and headed the page *Billy*.

'Contract out on him?' she said. 'Or shall we just nail his bollocks to a convent wall ourselves?'

Flower laughed in a slightly restrained way. 'I think we should talk to him,' she shouted over the hoover as it rattled and spat out some dangerous-looking smoke, indignant at being asked to suck up the debris of a good month's worth of crap.

'What, tell him to stop it and see if he does so like a good little boy?' shouted back Martha, who was down on her hands and knees with the Lump pressed rather uncomfortably against the carpet scooping up newspapers, cups with varying degrees of penicillin-like growth in them and a couple of pairs of very unattractive knickers that would get her stoned to death in a lap-dancing club.

'No need to be sarky,' said Flower. 'I'm sure we could get somewhere if we talked to him—correction, *I* could get somewhere. You'd probably make him go out and spray some puppies with automatic fire you wind him up so much.'

'All right then,' said Martha, 'you have a nice little chat with him, put him bang to rights and if it cures him of his violent tendencies, I'll clean the bath.'

Flower's resolve to sort Billy out strengthened.

'What do you think Sarah will think of us interfering?' she asked.

'We won't tell her,' said Martha, whose inclination was always towards the cloak and dagger.

'Really?' said Flower, who nearly had a mental

77

breakdown if she had to tell a lie.

'Look, she won't thank us. He won't tell her we've talked to him because he'll be too embarrassed. It's better all round to keep it quiet.'

'Oh my God!' said Flower.

'What?' said Martha and turned to see Flower gagging on account of an elderly plate of half-eaten dinner she'd discovered under a pile of mother and baby magazines.

'Look, shall we go down the caff and call it a day here?' Martha suggested, surveying the barely touched flat.

'Please,' said Flower.

They sat in Martha's local caff which surprisingly for the area was run by two very healthy people who served very healthy food—which meant that no one went in there very much.

The Sorting Out Billy list grew and moved from Flower and then Martha chatting to Billy to some slightly more duplicitous and then downright mad suggestions.

'How about trying to split them up?' offered Martha.

'But they love each other,' said Flower.

'What, in a Henry the Eighth-Anne Boleyn sort of a way, do you mean? Look, he's popped her one twice now and it's not going to stop, so if the gentle approach doesn't work we need some stand-by ideas.'

'Well, how could we split them up? I don't see,' said Flower.

'Easy peasy,' said Martha. 'You or I could sleep with him.'

'But Sarah would never talk to us again,' Flower objected.

'Yeh, but at least she would be able to talk . . . because she'd be alive.'

'Oh, don't be so melodramatic,' said Flower. 'He won't kill her, this is real life.'

'Yes, and ordinary people do things like this to each other,' said Martha grimly.

'What about just finding Sarah a new bloke?' said Flower.

'Sarah doesn't want a new bloke, she wants Billy.'

'OK, how about getting someone to threaten him?' This was an unusual and somewhat daring suggestion from a natural peacekeeper like Flower.

'Mmm, not a bad idea,' said Martha, 'but we'd have to get someone decent to really scare the shit out of him.'

'As opposed to . . . ?'

'Well, Charlie, or my dad,' said Martha. 'How about if we just go and buy a gun, get him in a room, point it at him and say, "Leave our friend alone or you lose your fucking crown jewels".'

They looked at each other and laughed uproariously.

CHAPTER NINE

In the end it was decided that both Flower and Martha would start the process of sorting things out for Sarah by talking to Billy and it fell to Flower as the natural conciliator to have the first attempt. She decided she would phone Billy at work so Sarah didn't find out what they were up to and then realised she had no idea where Billy

79

worked.

She got straight on the phone to Martha.

'Oh, it's some firm up in Whitechapel,' said Martha. 'Where all the killers come from.'

'Eh?' said Flower.

'Oh, a spurious reference to Jack the Ripper,' said Martha.

'No, he *killed* in Whitechapel, he didn't *come* from there.'

'How do you know?'

'Well, first of all, no one knows who he is so how would they know where he came from, and secondly—'

'Don't bother with secondly,' said Martha. 'I'm not that entertained by stories of prostitute murderers.'

'Ooh, you big fat feminist rebel,' said Flower.

'Anyway, I've got Billy's number,' said Martha. 'Got a pen?'

Flower gritted her teeth and dialled. She was hoping to get Billy's voicemail, but he picked it up.

'Hello, Bill Taylor speaking.'

'Bill, it's Flower,' said Flower.

There was a small pause during which Billy took in the information that one of his girlfriend's friends had called him at work. Within a split second he had speculated that she either wanted to sleep with him or shop him.

'And what can I do for you?' said Billy.

Flower hated that phrase. In her head she said, 'You can't do anything, you bad fucker, it's what I can do for you in terms of transforming you into a decent member of society.' She actually said, 'I want to have a chat with you about something. Can you meet me?'

'Very mysterious,' said Billy.

'I'm doing a gig on Wednesday at Frogs Wine Bar,' said Flower. 'Can you meet me there before it starts, about seven?'

'Give us a clue,' said Billy.

'No, I'll tell you when I see you,' said Flower and hung up.

'Who was that?' said Charlie, his radar bringing him prematurely from the bathroom.

'Oh, no one,' said Flower. 'Wrong number.'

Charlie wondered why Flower was even bothering with that lie because nobody ever believes that 'wrong number' line, but for once he let it go and sauntered into the kitchen to make some evil-looking, evil-smelling and evil-tasting tea.

Flower was slightly put out that he didn't give her the third degree. Perhaps he's saving it for the anger management group, she thought, which was where he was going the night she was meeting Billy.

Flower's heart thumped at the thought of it all going wrong with Billy, the gig falling apart and Charlie going mad when he found out that she had met Billy and talked to him on her own.

Why was life always such a worry? Why couldn't it be relaxing, fun and unchallenging? It was so much easier to do nothing than get involved in other people's problems. Flower thought of a saying her father was constantly trumpeting at her as a child, as she was dragged on yet another demonstration heading towards Hyde Park. He used to say, 'For evil to triumph it is necessary only for good men to do nothing.' Well, what a pain *that* was! Why couldn't it be, 'For goodness to triumph it is necessary only for good men to sit on their arses and get pissed'? Why was poking your nose

81

into other people's problems always at such a high emotional cost?

* * *

Wednesday arrived with the unsettling speed of a teenage mugger, as do all days which engender apprehension of some sort, and Flower found herself walking towards Frogs Wine Bar going through her lines for her guest spot.

The man behind the Frogs empire of one sad lonely club had decided to jump on the comedy bandwagon with very little idea of where he was going; the facilities, as usual, were not at their best. There was no changing room and Flower couldn't believe it when the choice put to her was the women's toilet—one smelly cubicle—or standing on the pavement outside.

Flower clocked Marty Mavers in the women's toilet, a highly ambitious Australian comic who kept a record of hers and everyone else's earnings and had her nose so far up the arses of the relevant TV people that, had her nose been the size of Flower's, their livers and kidneys would have been shredded. So Flower decided she'd stand out on the pavement with Dunk, a Cambridge university graduate who believed there was far more danger and excitement to be had amongst the comedy clubs of London than on some adventure trail in South America, much to his parents' disappointment as they had very little else to do with their money, their imaginations being inversely proportional to their wealth.

Billy found Dunk and Flower chatting just as it started to rain so he and Flower escaped inside to

82

Meanwhile, Flower's heart had been broken as she'd been forced off the stage by the heckler and there was nowhere to run except the ladies' toilets where Marty Mavers stood, combining the incongruity of a smug grin and a tragic voice full of empathy about Flower's demise.

'It all takes time,' she said, sounding like some teacher Flower had hated at school and Flower felt a rising inclination to thump her silly face. Instead she said, 'Thanks, Marty,' flatly and turned to leave.

As she did so, an audience member appeared in the doorway and said, 'I thought you were great!'

'Thanks,' said Marty, extending a hand.

'I'm sorry,' said the punter, 'I didn't mean you, I meant her.'

Flower was so grateful she could have cried and with her head held high she left the toilet, somewhat repaired, leaving a foolish-looking Marty Mavers wondering why the only punter in the whole room who could possibly prefer Flower's act to hers, had walked into their toilet.

On her way out, the club-owner Tom stopped Flower and for one joyful moment Flower thought he would offer her a booking. It wasn't to be. He handed her a note.

'Someone likes you,' he said.

Flower opened the note. It was from the heckler, she deduced cleverly as it was signed *The Heckler*, and it said:

This time the victory is mine but if you are very, very, very nice to me, I'll leave you alone. More instructions to follow.

Flower shivered. Oh great, she thought. This is

just what I need. She chucked the note away thinking that if Charlie saw it, it might set back all the good work done by anger management.

If only.

All the good work done by anger management consisted of a bloody nose, bruised spine and torn trousers for Charlie. As he and Flower limped home from opposite points of the compass, each damaged in different ways, both feeling utterly defeated, Martha's voice was flying over their heads along a wire to Sarah who, revelling in the luxury of a night in on her own with no fear of saying the wrong thing or being clumsy or burning the dinner, was chatting happily on the phone with her, about the mess that was their romantic lives.

'Look, Marth, I love him so I'm hardly going to walk away, am I?' said Sarah, sounding like a girl band.

'But Sar, you've got to think of yourself in this,' said Martha. 'I know you underplay it 'cause you're embarrassed, but be honest, are you scared of him?'

'Sometimes,' Sarah said, underplaying 'almost all the time' to something more palatable.

'Well, is that a good basis for a relationship?' said Martha.

'It's better than not having one at all,' said Sarah, touching on one of life's great questions for many women who feel like a spare part-cum-leper if they are not accompanied by a penis-owner at all times.

'Oh thanks,' said Martha. 'Thanks for reminding me.'

'You've got the Lump,' said Sarah, who truly believed that it was possible for a baby to fill a relationship-sized gap.

'I can't fuck the baby,' said Martha crossly and then thought how lucky it was that her father couldn't listen in to her conversations any more.

'Marth, what a terrible thing to say,' said Sarah.

'Sorry,' said Martha grudgingly. She had got so used to winding up her dad, it leaked into other parts of her life too.

Tentatively, Sarah said, 'Look, Marth, you haven't told anyone who the father of Lump is yet. We want to help, you know. Why won't you tell us?'

Martha had been caught at a rather hormonal time by Sarah and her resolve, like some tuberculosis-ridden Victorian heroine, to keep schtumm about the origins of the Lump, caved in and she started to weep great big hiccuppy sobs down the phone.

'Oh, I'm sorry,' said Sarah. 'I didn't mean to set you off.'

'I don't know!' wailed Martha through a wall of snot.

'Don't know what?' said Sarah. 'Don't know what to do?'

'No, don't know who the father is,' lied Martha.

'Well, how many possibles are there?' said Sarah.

'Three,' said Martha.

'Bloody hell!' said Sarah. 'I never realised.'

'I'm so embarrassed,' said Martha as she sobbed on.

'Can't you do one of them tests?' said Sarah. 'Who are they, anyway?'

'Look, I can't talk now,' said Martha. 'I'm dying for a piss. I'll meet you and Flower in the pub and tell you all about it.'

'Don't worry,' said Sarah. 'It'll be all right,'

although she had no more idea whether it would be than whether Flower would make it on the comedy circuit, something she had assured her of many times.

'I'd better go,' said Martha. 'See you tomorrow night?'

Sarah didn't want to say, 'If it's all right with Billy,' but Martha sensed that this was an issue and said, 'If not then, Friday eh?' knowing Billy went out with workmates on Friday nights.

Sarah went to bed that night with a list of names in her head about who the most likely candidates could be and found herself, strangely, to be somewhat envious of Martha's predicament.

As she dropped off, she narrowed the list down to four and was eager to see if any of them were right. There was Martha's ex-boyfriend Alan the Planet, so named because his head contained many more facts than most people's. He'd moved away and the relationship had lost impetus as his visits got less frequent. Or could it be Martha's next-door neighbour, fourteen-year-old Junior, with whom she flirted outrageously whenever she got the chance? Perhaps it was Ted, her boss from work, whose unattractiveness was negated by a large wallet and a wicked sense of humour, or maybe that bloke whose name she couldn't remember whom they'd met in a club in East London.

Her money was on Ted.

CHAPTER ELEVEN

Charlie and Flower sat miserably at home like a pair of pensioners who'd just discovered rationing was back. They were hunched over a small electric fire because the central heating had broken down and the weatherman had been excitable to the point of idiocy as he described the coming cold snap. Charlie, as is common in enough men for women to comment on, was hypochondriacal to the point of having cheated death many times in his head and was swathed in hot towels with a Lemsip and Marijuana Sprinkle, as he called it, to dull the physical pain brought on by the anger management group. Flower, on the other hand, was suffering a higher form of pain, the emotional humiliation of the heckled-off comic which makes one feel like one's insides have been taken out and auctioned off outside the local newsagent for enemies to use as table decorations.

At that moment, Hitler ('so we never forget the evil bastard existed' . . . Charlie Knapp 1992), their black and white cat, entered the room, limping, with one of his back legs in plaster completing the sad trio of damaged creatures in the house. Had Charlie and Flower been a little less depressed the cat would have offered the possibility of a good laugh at themselves, a route untravelled by too many politicians and celebrities.

Charlie had related his tale of woe from anger management and was trying to explain to Flower that with such a volatile group he didn't think it was the best idea to send Billy along quite yet.

Flower then related the tragic tale of her evening, leaving out the Billy and heckler elements because they would have upset Charlie, which meant he found it difficult to understand why it had been such a bad evening.

'Oh, let's do it,' said Charlie, which was his answer to pretty much any traumatic situation and Flower thought fondly of the times she had been pinned to the ground by him in the midst of some chaos—a demo that went wrong at Stonehenge, under a police van, round at her parents' just after an emotional dinner and their most unusual perhaps, a quick one in Sainsburys at two in the morning over the organic frozen section. It was quite difficult to make it look like they were taking a long time to decide whether to go for veggie sausage rolls or a turkey that had had a damn good run round a bit of mud in Essex before it was pulverised. Normally in a relationship the sexual urge cools unevenly, but in Flower and Charlie's case even after many years together there was an equal appetite not only for the long slow encounter but also the race against Big Ben's bongs for the midday news.

This time it was on the floor in their scruffy living room, and if either of them had been interested they would have spotted the flash of binoculars as their neighbour opposite, a long-time silent participator in their sex-life, thanked his lucky stars for a grandstand view and put the phone down rather abruptly on the local radio station before his voice rose too highly. Another skill Flower and Charlie possessed was the ability to discuss any aspect of their life, however trivial, during fucking—so the conversation about Billy's

96

90 per cent of the population when driving, she assumed that she could access a message and read it quite safely whilst continuing to pedal home through the cheerless South London night. Of course, Flower pressed a wrong button, tried to peer more closely at her phone and careered off the road and up onto the kerb which flipped her off and she landed on her bum on the pavement. More embarrassed than hurt, and cursing Charlie who had obviously decided to encourage her home for their tryst textually, she found the message.

Two nil it said, followed by a capital H, and it was enough to let the Grim Reaper clutch her heart and give it a good squeeze as she realised it was from the heckler. How did he have her phone number? This was getting spooky and she didn't like it. Perhaps she'd better tell Charlie. Well, at least she could tell the girls and see what they said although their advice, from the heavily pregnant, hormonally flooded Martha to the emotional knife-edge that was Sarah, might not be worth having at the moment.

'All right, love?' shouted a voice. 'That's not a chair, you know!'

She looked over to see a leering greasy sort of face poking out of an estate car. Fucking hell, she thought. I'm still being heckled. 'More's the pity, or I could ram a leg up your arse,' she replied and shuddered at her own creative limits.

The driver looked mortally wounded, as a lot of street hecklers do if you actually come back at them . . . well, either that or they stab you and it was Flower's lucky night.

Back at home, Charlie's erection had faded, been reactivated by a quick five minutes of his

Mary Poppins video and then died again when Flower phoned him to say she'd come off her bike. They had an early sleep-filled night.

*   *   *

On Friday night the King's Head received Martha, Flower and Sarah into its dankness like little sperms into a big womb. The air was foetid and smoke hung in the air but they all loved it like a mangy old dog that refused to die.

Flower and Sarah were shivery with anticipation as they were about to find out who the father of the Lump was, a most unexpected development and one which they had assumed wouldn't happen until the Lump was about five and someone made a drunken slip of the tongue at a party.

Martha had steeled herself with a few drinks, knowing she shouldn't but this was a four-fag emergency and at least she hadn't given in and smoked, but as the Bloody Marys slipped down, she mused that at least she was introducing some Vitamin C along with the foetal alcohol syndrome. She regretted having to tell Sarah and Flower the truth, as she had rather enjoyed being a woman of mystery for eight months while they and her relatives pondered the gritty question of who could have impregnated her, and it had to be said that the Rev Brian had mooted the idea with Pat that someone had perhaps forced himself onto their daughter.

The etiquette for revealing to your two best friends the identity of the father of your soon-to-be-born child is not described anywhere in a manual so none of them really knew what to do.

110

ground her foot into Martha's under the table. Martha began to laugh hysterically. 'Ha! Ha! Only joking!' she said. Flower joined in with as natural a laugh as she could manage, which wasn't very.

Flower's mobile started to ring. Perhaps the only occasion it had managed such perfect timing. 'Excuse me,' she said.

It was Charlie at the other end to tell her someone from the Nightcap had phoned to ask where she was.

'Oh piss,' said Flower, 'I've got to go. I forgot I had a gig tonight.' She gathered everything in a flurry of roll-up tobacco smoke and jasmine perfume and headed out of the door in a huge panic, throwing, 'See you over the weekend!' behind her as she sailed out.

'I can see when I'm not wanted as well, girls' talk and all that,' said Billy. 'See you later. And don't be too late, Sarah, will you?' He disappeared into the gloom.

'What did you do that for?' said Sarah.

'What?' said Martha, whose short-term memory would have been seen by a geriatrician as definite proof of the onset of Alzheimer's. Then: 'Oh, sometimes I just get sick of pretending everything's all right with you two,' she snapped. 'He's a bully.'

'He's got his own problems,' said Sarah.

'Oh yeh? Tell me about them,' said Martha.

'I'd better go,' said Sarah.

'Oh come on,' said Martha, 'there's another half hour's drinking time left and we can't fall out over a bloke.'

'We're not,' lied Sarah, 'but I've just got to go.'

Martha, who often thought in visual clichés, saw in her mind a big wedge being hammered in and its

115

thin end disappearing under a door.

'All right,' she said brightly. 'We'll talk over the weekend?' It was half confident statement, half question.

Sarah headed slowly home hoping Billy wasn't going to be in a mood. She got home and Billy wasn't even there.

Martha was left with her sparkling water, which she swigged back, making a hideous face, and off she went.

*   *   *

Flower got to the Nightcap in quite a short time as she had flown through all the traffic-lights on her bike causing many simmering motorists to shout abuse after her disappearing form. She wanted to stop and explain she didn't normally do it, but needed to talk herself into a horrible sarcastic comedy mood, so she turned back and tried to give them a dirty look, something some women just aren't very good at, especially if they are nice and middle class. Flower would no sooner dream of screaming abuse after anyone than killing them with a gun.

On with Flower that night at the Nightcap were Dick Knob and Will Hatchard. Dick Knob was on last and Flower before him. Will Hatchard was doing well when she arrived. He was a Liverpudlian whose naturally drooping moustachio-ed face suited comedy very well and his heckle put-downs were generally agreed to be so good that almost everyone else was doing them.

'Have you ever wanted to kill anyone?' Flower asked Dick as they sat in the dingy dressing-room through the dirty window of which they could just see feet and ankles going about their business in late-night Soho.

'Only a twelve year old who wouldn't suck me off,' said Dick, who often spoke as if he was onstage.

'No, seriously,' said Flower.

'Why? Do you want to kill someone?' said the unusually perceptive Dick.

'I felt like it earlier,' said Flower. 'Sometimes I really wish I had a gun . . . just to frighten them, you know.'

'Who's them?' said Dick.

'Oh, arseholes, that sort,' said Flower.

'I'll get you a gun if that's what you want, sweetheart,' said Dick, trying Humphrey Bogart and getting an old American stroke victim instead.

'You're kidding,' said Flower, open-mouthed.

'Not at all,' said Dick. 'You want to come with me down Canning Town tomorrow, I'll talk to some mates.'

Flower felt slightly unreal as though it wasn't really her talking. 'No, it's all right,' she said. 'It'd be mad.'

'Oh come on,' said Dick, 'it'll be a laugh. Then you can blow Charlie's head off.'

'It's not Charlie who pisses me off,' said Flower.

This pissed Dick off because he had fancied Flower for ages even though she was so different from the sort of woman he normally went for, brassy and not fussy.

'Whatever,' said Dick.

'I don't know,' said Flower, feeling icy.

'Well, give us a call on the mobile tomorrow if you fancy it,' said Dick.

CHAPTER FOURTEEN

'Oh, somebody shoot her, please!'

A wave of laughter soared across the darkened room, hitting a demoralised Flower with the realisation that she wasn't a very sharp comic tonight, her self-esteem was starting to burrow through to Australia, and The Heckler was back. Yes, she had given him capital letters finally and it was obligatory for him now to torture her mentally before, in the final showdown, she rid the world of him, as a heckler not a person, she hastily added to herself. Being funny isn't something most people do consistently. Everyone has off days and the greatest fear of the comic is that the comedy muse will leave them sweating with fear in their unmade bed and fly into the mind of their greatest rival, raising his comedy skills to even greater heights.

Flower drooped and the audience actually began to feel sorry for her, but she hadn't learned to use that sympathy either and after a couple more stabs at put-downs which sounded like she was addressing a slightly irritable latecomer at a knitting circle, Flower gave up again and headed off the stage.

'I'll get the cunt for you,' said the ever-chivalrous Dick Knob as they passed in the tiny corridor.

'Thanks,' said Flower miserably.

'Right, where's that heckler?' said Dick Knob as he stepped onstage. 'It's a long time since I penetrated the arsehole of an arsehole.'

The crowd woofed with delight. They could feel he was in control and Flower crept to the back to

118

'It's fucking Laurel and Hardy,' said one and the others cackled like a hen-night posse. Flower and Martha quickened their pace and the girls, hungry for more excitement than teasing two women in their thirties, moved on.

'Do you think anyone ever shouts compliments when they heckle people in the street?' wondered Flower.

' 'Course they do,' said Martha. 'Stuff like, "Nice tits!" or, "Give you one!"'

'No, I don't really mean that,' said Flower. 'I'm talking more about something like, "Oh, you look like a nice friendly person who treats the rest of the human race as your equal".'

'Oh, come on, Flower,' said Martha.

'But why are all heckles negative and horrible?'

'You said heckles, that's not really what you get on the street.'

'Yes, it is. Pooh.'

Martha held her nose and her stomach heaved as they hurried past a big bank of bins which were being rifled through by a homeless person.

'Got any change, love?' he asked.

Flower began to shuffle through her pockets and found a pound.

'Cheers, darling,' said the man happily as though this wasn't a bitterly cold night, he wasn't dressed in filthy clothes and he didn't sleep nightly on a bed of dog shit.

'You're welcome,' smiled Flower, looking sickeningly beatific and, if she was honest with herself, feeling it too. The mood changed.

'Well fuck you, you patronising cow,' he shouted, throwing the coin onto the pavement with such rage that Flower and Martha were quite frightened.

'Come on,' said Flower and bent over to pick it up, at which point the man rather unceremoniously vomited on her back.

'Jesus Christ,' wailed Flower.

The man threw his head back, laughed like a demented clown and headed off into the night.

Martha was having trouble holding the contents of her own stomach in check as she dabbed ineffectually at her friend's back with half a crumpled tissue. Flower was filled with a by-now familiar wave of urban hatred.

'I could kill that old bastard,' she said.

'Ah, but could you?' said Martha, philosophical for a moment.

'If I had a gun,' said Flower, 'I'd soon put him out of his misery.'

'But he was quite happy until you did a Mother Teresa on him,' said Martha.

'No, I didn't,' said Flower.

'Did,' said Martha.

'Well, I'm just sick of being a perfectly ordinary, reasonably pleasant person and getting shit all the time,' said Flower. 'On the street, in the clubs, even at work . . . by these people who quite honestly don't deserve to take up the space they do on the planet.'

'I know what you mean, but who are we to decide?' said Martha. 'I'd like to shoot that Billy through the block and tackle, but I don't want to go to prison and ultimately I don't want to ruin Sarah's life.'

'You might make her life,' said Flower, 'and let's be honest, our judgement is probably less flawed than your average Middle Eastern dictator.'

'Well,' said Martha, 'if you had a chance to disappear Billy off the face of the earth, would you do it?'

'You bet I would, man,' said Flower, who couldn't help lapsing into hippy vernacular from time to time, 'and I might be able to.'

She told Martha about Dick Knob's offer and Martha found herself encouraging her to at least go and get a gun, the power of it appealed so much to her, and as they walked along the dirty streets, she visualised several urban scenes in which she would threaten people and make them behave the way *she* wanted—finishing with a lovely scenario involving the Reverend Brian.

The night bus approached and the two women climbed on, going to the top deck so Martha could sniff the cigarette smoke of the alcohol-fuelled disobedients on top. This was a foolish mistake, because that night, like most nights, the night bus had become the transport of the Grim Reaper on his day off and was filled with a selection of the most unnerving and unpleasant individuals you could imagine, from barely conscious dribblers to groups of teenage boys with their young offender hats on. Flower and Martha huddled down into their seats, but the incident earlier made Flower somewhat of a nasal target.

'What is that stink?' enquired a teenager and elicited for some reason hysterical laughter from his mates.

'It's them two,' he said, pointing a finger at Flower and Martha. This was a cue for everyone else on the bus to breathe a sigh of relief and look out of the window while Martha and Flower got murdered or whatever.

CHAPTER FIFTEEN

Being surrounded by a group of teenagers who have imbibed a selection of more imaginative substances than alcohol and drugs was not an ideal finish to the night.

These days, thought Martha, the contents of a chemistry lab were available to any kid from his friendly street-corner dealer for the price of a packet of fags, so God knew what biochemical imbalances were propelling their anti-social behaviour tonight.

One aspect of travelling in a big city at night is the reassuring knowledge that, should a situation get out of hand, no one will lift a finger to help. Numerous excuses flit through people's heads, all of them centring on the fact that risking injury for another human being you haven't even met just isn't worth it.

Knowing this made Flower feel very vulnerable indeed, and because of Martha's pregnant state she knew she would be called upon to defend her. She also knew that neither of them was attractive enough to warrant a front-page report in the paper if they were injured or killed, because it was required that you looked vaguely like a model if you got murdered. It was hard luck but, as a nation, nobody mourns the passing of the less attractive citizen unless they are important in some way. Flower decided to take responsibility and try the pacifist approach.

'Look, it's me who smells,' she explained apologetically like a Sunday-school teacher. 'A man was sick on me, right?'

One would have thought this was the funniest thing the gang had ever heard, as they indulged in hugely exaggerated laughing, rolling in the aisle, poking each other and generally swaggering around intimidating others with their laughter. The leader of the gang, however, sat in the middle of them, his pasty, impassive face belying an IQ of 140 and a wish to study medicine. Held back from achieving his goal by his unpleasant personality and parents who thought being a doctor was 'poofy', he made up his mind. 'Well, I don't like the smell. Let's get her off the fucking bus.'

The laughing stopped as it dawned on the fringe members of the gang, who were no more than overgrown ten year olds, what they were being asked to do. They knew disobeying this pizza base on legs would result in some sort of violence towards them and they would rather risk injuring someone by throwing them down some bus stairs than incurring his wrath. A few of them began to edge like cringing dogs towards Flower. Flower panicked and said things like, 'It's all right, I'll just go,' but she realised that they intended to have some sport with her whatever she said or did.

Martha was also aware that things were looking dodgy and tried to out-bravado the weaker teenagers.

'Come on, you little shits,' she said, trying to look relaxed. 'Pick on someone your own size i.e. someone smaller than me,' realising too late that the 'i.e.' was a bad idea and had only confused them.

The fringe members looked hesitantly at their leader, whose glare was unflinching, and realised they would have to do his bidding.

Martha's hand tightened round a Swiss army knife she kept in her handbag, fumbling for the blade and unfortunately coaxing out the bit that removed stones from horses' hooves. I'm sure that'll come in handy with one of these donkeys, she thought grimly to herself. She felt the Lump jump and twist inside her. Someone's up for a fight, she noted.

As the gang advanced, Flower started doing a sort of low whimpering that couldn't be heard by anyone except Martha.

'Don't worry,' said Martha. 'We'll be OK. Something'll turn up.'

Everyone else on the bus was listening to every word and holding their breath, and a few communicated desperately with their eyes to their partners. A middle-aged couple on holiday from America knew full well the consequences of intervening, having tried it in New York and been beaten for their troubles; a younger couple from South London who had just got engaged simultaneously decided they didn't want to be stabbed on a bus before their wedding for the sake of a hippy covered in sick. Four drunk students knew enough of London Transport to keep their lips buttoned, and a slightly older but smaller gang of teenagers knew they were outnumbered and stared resolutely ahead.

That left, sitting quietly at the front of the bus waiting patiently for his moment and equipped to deal with this situation physically and mentally, a certain Mr Michael Randall who spent many a Friday night sitting expectantly on the night bus waiting for things to erupt. Up to this point they never had and it was ironic, he thought to himself, that he was being called up as a gallant knight for these two unfortunate-looking girls who had recently joined his self-defence class. He had not acknowledged himself to them, in fact he never did to anyone when he was on one of his jaunts, just in case he had to hit them or humiliate himself in front of them.

It would be reassuring to report that Michael Randall rose magnificently from his seat and stood at the top of the bus, eyes blazing and weapons poised, but he was too weaselly for that. He just sort of slimed to his feet and with the anger of ten men launched himself screaming towards the fracas, something he had read was essential to terrify the enemy, from the rebel yell of the Confederates in the American Civil War to the blood-freezing roar of the raggle-taggle Scots at Culloden.

The teenagers were truly shocked that what appeared to be a skinny, human version of Golem had decided to take them on and felt confident that Ant, the one with the biggest punch, could take him out. Before Ant could manage this though, Michael Randall had all but blinded him with two fingers poked without mercy into his eyes. Ant fell to the ground screaming and holding his face.

Drama queen, thought Martha.

Spurred on by this vicious assault on their manhood by a stoat in a car coat, Ant's mates Jez and Luca took their chances. Jez took a swing at Michael Randall, missed and received a size eight in the bollocks, perfectly placed with a terrible force. He too hit the deck screaming. Luca pulled out a knife and held it gleaming for a split second before Michael Randall took it from him in one deft move and brought it down into his thigh. This made Martha wince at the memory of trying to open a toffee tin on the bus as a schoolgirl with her compasses and stabbing herself in the leg.

The gang thought that safety in numbers was the only answer now and Dom, Lob and Taz, who sounded like three forwards for Charlton Atheltic, broadsided Michael Randall in an attempt to get him on the floor and kick the crap out of him. But Michael Randall had lived this scenario too many times in his head to get it wrong at this point and, bringing out a rounders bat ('more easily concealed, thicker and more convenient to handle'), he played their heads like a xylophone until they retreated down the steps at the end of the bus wondering why they felt like cuddling their mums, who had given them nothing but grief since they were little kids.

This left the gang leader Moz alone and seething as his lieutenants fell around him and he sat trying to sneer as Michael approached, confident even despite the carnage, that he could handle whatever this little man chose to throw at him.

But Michael Randall had something special for Moz. Within seconds he had whipped out what looked like a helmet, around which he had attached a band of metal which could be tightened. Before he knew what had happened, Moz sat with a kitchen colander on his head as Michel deftly tightened it and threw the Allen key out of the window. It was snug enough to hurt a lot but not to do any damage, and as he strolled back down the bus and winked at Martha and Flower, the whole bus erupted into laughter as a pained-looking Moz

'We've got the sublime and the ridiculous here,' she said, 'from talking to him to trying to split them up, to trying to turn Sarah into a lesbian, to a contract killing, to tampering with the brakes on his car.'

'Oh yeah—and you'd know how to do the brakes on his car, would you?' said Flower.

'I would, actually,' said Martha, 'seeing as when I lived in the village I knocked around with a mechanic for quite a while.'

'Did you ever find out anything useful?' said Flower.

'Such as?'

'Oh, you know, how to change a wheel, that sort of thing.'

'Oh Christ no, nothing that dull,' said Martha.

'So let's do his brakes,' Flower heard herself say and then laughed at how odd it sounded. Martha began to laugh too and they were nearly onto the guffawing stage when the phone rang. Considering it was one in the morning, both girls felt their hearts leap and each separately wondered whether Billy could have heard them and was phoning to threaten them.

It was Charlie.

'It's only Charlie,' said Flower with her hand over the receiver because she knew he would be offended by the 'only', and in their relief, they began to laugh.

'What's going on?' said Charlie irritatedly, assuming he was being discussed and laughed at.

'Nothing,' said Flower, always an unsatisfactory reply.

'When are you coming home?' said Charlie.

Flower felt like saying, 'When you change the fucking record,' but in fact said, 'Not long now.'

'Look, I'll come and get you,' said Charlie. 'Be there in twenty-five.' As usual Flower had no time to agree to this.

Martha, serious for a moment, said, 'Look—if Billy doesn't settle down with Sarah and increase his battering in direct proportion to how long they are together, he'll just do it to someone else.'

'I know,' said Flower, 'but it's not our job. One in four women suffer domestic violence, but we can't kill a quarter of the blokes in the country.'

'It *is* our job,' said Martha.

'Why?' said Flower.

'Because we're pissed as farts,' Martha replied, starting to roar with laughter again and wetting herself slightly in the process, because of the pressure of Lump. She didn't tell Flower. Oh God, thought Martha, I am pissed and I'm about to have a baby. I must be more sensible. And this made her laugh even more. She bent double and headed for the toilet, trying to stop any more urine leaking out. On the way back, she noticed that Flower had taken up Martha's list and was adding some things. Rudely, she snatched it from her. 'Therapy?' she read dismissively. 'Waste of bloody money and effort.'

'I'm not getting into the therapy argument again with you,' said Flower.

'And what's this,' said Martha. 'Anger fucking management?'

'You need fucking swearing management,' said Flower.

'Oh, come on though,' said Martha. 'A load of violent wankers sitting round in a circle saying, "And then I hit her with a hammer", what bloody good is that going to do?'

134

room, go and look.'

'What is it, bucket of water on the door?' said Charlie. 'Blow up doll in the bed?'

'No, it's my bloody mother and don't wake her,' Martha told him.

Charlie wandered into the room and could just make out a shape under the bedclothes which he assumed was made up of pillows. He sat down on the edge of the bed and gave the shape a good prod.

'Hello Martha's mum, you old slapper,' he said.

A hand appeared from under the duvet and grabbed his groin area and he nearly went through the ceiling. The look on his face as he arrived back in the room with Martha and Flower told them he'd found Pat and that she'd found him. Martha also had a colander on her head.

'Come on, Flower,' said Charlie, 'time to go home.'

For once Flower didn't argue.

*   *   *

The following morning everyone had a hangover except Sarah who had gone to bed early and woke up feeling refreshed and healthy. She decided as Billy lay snoring, not something one expects handsome men to indulge in, that she would wander down to Martha's, have a coffee and see how the Lump was coming along, and try to pump her for some more details of the Ted encounter.

Martha looked bloody awful, a mop of greasy hair perched on top of a sallow face with two bloodshot eyes the only splash of colour. 'What time is it?' she said in a voice reminiscent of a frog.

137

'About ten, mate,' said Sarah. 'Put the kettle on, I'm dying for a coffee.'

Martha's hideous appearance was further emphasised by the fact that Sarah looked like a Swiss milkmaid in the complexion department. Martha went to put the kettle on and shouted various bits of conversation through to where Sarah was sitting, not really noticing that she wasn't answering but occasionally 'umming' or grunting. Martha made her coffee in a cup whose contents looked a couple of days old and did Sarah the honour of rinsing hers under a warm tap.

'Flower had a terrible heckler last night,' she said as she carried the coffees into the room and realised that Sarah had a very angry expression reminiscent of the Rev Brian on her face.

'What the fuck is this?' she demanded, waving a pad at Martha.

'It's a pad, dear,' said Martha.

'And what is this list on it?' said Sarah.

Martha realised in a millionth of a second that it was her and Flower's list for sorting out Billy. Did it have his name on it? Or had she torn it off? Was he identifiable from the different suggestions? She took a gamble.

'Oh, I'm writing a book at work,' she said.

'Bullshit,' said Sarah. 'It's about Bill, isn't it?'

'What makes you say that?'

'I can just tell,' said Sarah.

Great, thought Martha. It hasn't got his name on then. 'Look,' she said aloud. 'I don't really want to . . . that is, I'm a bit embarrassed—well, you'll find out sooner or later. My mum's here and my dad's been knocking her about.'

'No!' Sarah was astounded. She thought the Rev

138

Brian only had a bark.

'Don't say anything if she comes in,' said Martha, 'but Flower and I were pissed last night and we made a list of how we could help my mum.'

As if summoned to explain herself, Pat appeared at the door with Martha's dressing-gown over her clothes looking drained of blood.

'I'm sorry, dear. I think I might have been drunk last night,' Pat said. 'It won't happen again.'

CHAPTER SEVENTEEN

While Sarah was round at Martha's, Billy was at home watching a Saturday-morning football programme on television. A piece of his mind, however, and not the bit he always gave Sarah, was on something else. It wasn't sex, although men apparently think about it every seven seconds. Who researched that particular statistic? Billy wondered. Who was their control group and wouldn't men just say they were thinking about sex, rather than owning up to musings on scaffolding, say, or macramé?

Billy had decided recently that he really, really liked Sarah, could tolerate her weird friends and could quite happily settle for this life he had with her. He had all but given up the adolescent hope of the leggy model/porn star/actress with exploding bosoms beckoning to him in a bar one night and thought at the age of thirty-two he should probably be sensible and squirt his semen into a permanent seedbed. However, like most men, a tiny bit of him clung onto the vain hope that even though he was happy in a relationship which made him want, for the first time, to sort out his violent temper, especially when drinking, he could still make room in his sexual calendar for a dirty woman. Why do my thoughts always sound like a bad porn film? he asked himself.

Billy, unlike some violent men, was aware of just how bad his bad behaviour was, knew it needed to be curtailed and wondered if there was any help for people like him. His violence couldn't be put to good use as a championship boxer or inner-city comprehensive deputy headmaster so he had better deal with it. Billy knew that when his temper started to mushroom, he became a thug; anyone, even someone he had decided he loved, could fan the flames and make him so full of rage that he questioned whether this deep-seated anger would ever go away. Maybe some poncy *Guardian*-reading arse from North London could guide him towards being a better person, but he doubted it. Billy couldn't help it that his critical voice was directed outwards, towards others, whereas most women's are directed inwards. He would always find weaknesses in others; it was just a question of how he dealt with them.

As he lay on the settee thinking, Sarah opened the door and came in, calling out a greeting and dropping her bag on the hall table with a crash, which ever so slightly irritated Billy, who was still daydreaming. He thought about shouting something but checked himself. Sarah then clattered into the bathroom and he heard her running the shower and wondered whether she would leave the shower curtain outside the frame and get water on the floor, not to mention leaving the soap in a glutinous mess. He also wondered, briefly, why she was having a shower and within seconds had concocted a scenario in his head in which Sarah was being fucked up against a wall by a workmate of his called Craig, until he actually began to believe this scenario. He found himself dialling Craig's mobile number to see whether he was at home in Hertfordshire and, after a brief chat in which he invented a spurious reason for calling, wondered how Craig could have got home from this liaison so quickly.

Sarah, unaware of this ominous mind-ratcheting, was singing some dreadful song that was in the charts. This was one of the many things Billy didn't understand about Sarah and other women; she didn't have a favourite band, knew nothing about the people who performed the music she did like, had no inkling of back catalogues, who played saxophone on B sides and who managed bands through the difficult times. *And* she never put CDs away.

Sarah, in the meantime, was in the shower preparing for her usual beauty routine. Some girls do, some don't. The ones who don't can't be arsed and are irritated by the ones who do because it underlines their neglect of what has become, over the years, a fundamental girlie obligation. Martha, for example, thought cleansing, toning and moisturising was a waste of time and believed that advice from various cosmetic companies to do so was a ploy to scare women into a phobia about wrinkles, thereby forcing them into a continuous frenzy of beauty product acquisition. She told people she didn't buy beauty products on principle but, in fact, on a Saturday night would slap on the slap with the best of them. Flower didn't use anything and didn't need to, and her lack of beauty product use was based on the fact that she had been told by someone once that some beauty creams were made from the aborted foetuses of French nuns and try as she might to get this image out of her head, every attempt at moisturising evoked the unpleasant feeling that she was rubbing a baby into her cheek.

Sarah, however, was meticulous and spent hours at the beauty counters of the biggest department stores, weighing up the pros and cons of various products and listening intently to the generalised bullshit of the immaculately plastered women with their flawless foundations, huge panda eyes and encyclopaedic celebrity knowledge.

After rubbing in a sizeable amount of coconut oil when she left the shower, Sarah started from her feet and worked her way up using three different sprays to keep her fresh for feet, armpits and a spray that is euphemistically termed an 'intimate' deodorant because it masks the pungent smell of woman with an industrial-strength floweriness that can kill puppies at ten yards.

Sarah then tackled the problem of removing hair from the bits of her body it shouldn't be on, in her case legs, armpits and face. She was scrupulous about her face as she couldn't help associating moustaches with comic-book lesbians. This was perhaps because your average teenage street heckler did too and she lived in fear of being on her own or worse, with Billy, when the, 'Oi, like the 'tache!' heckle came, the consequences of which would be a hugely bruised ego or hugely bruised teenager. Sarah had tried hair removal creams but

unrelaxed, she said, 'What is the matter, Charlie?'

'He hit me,' said Charlie in a voice that demonstrated he was getting used to it.

'Who?' asked Flower, still not really listening.

'Billy Bloody Arseface Taylor, that's who,' said Charlie.

Finally Flower sat up and took notice. 'Billy hit you?'

'Yep,' said Charlie. 'Something weird was going on at that house of pain. I heard shouting and stuff being chucked, then I did my little speech and the bastard chinned me.'

'Did you see Sarah?'

'No, I can't say I did.'

'Well, did you hear her?'

'No,' Charlie admitted.

'So you don't know if she's dead or alive?'

'Oh, don't be such a drama queen,' said Charlie. 'Of course she isn't dead.'

Flower reached for the phone and dialled Sarah's number. Billy answered.

'Hello, can I speak to Sarah?' said Flower.

'No,' said Billy. 'She's not here.'

'Well, where is she?' Flower could hear the anxiety in her own voice.

'Gone shopping,' said Billy. 'I'll tell her you called.' He hung up.

'He's killed her,' said Flower. 'I'm going to call the police.'

'And what good are those fascist wankers going to do?' said Charlie.

Irritated, Flower said, 'This is not the time or the place for a rant about the police.'

'Nor is it time for a pre-menstrual fantasy about suburban murder either,' said Charlie, who

147

recognised the symptoms.

'I do not have PMS!' screamed Flower.

'We call it good old PMT in England, I think you'll find,' said Charlie, from whom anti-Americanism tempered with unwarranted chauvinism occasionally escaped.

'Call her mobile,' he suggested, so Flower did and Sarah answered sounding rather muted but perfectly alive.

'Are you all right?' asked Flower.

'Is Charlie all right?' countered Sarah. 'I'm really sorry.'

'Not your fault,' said Flower. 'Do you want to come round?'

'No, I'm out shopping. I'll buy a new skirt, I think, and that'll help.' Sarah had some insight into her shopping trips but only on a very superficial level. Flower always said if someone called it retail therapy once more to her face she would hit them, but Sarah wouldn't even know what retail therapy was.

'Did he hit you?'

'Only with a door and not on purpose.'

Flower's hormones dictated that more melodrama entered their conversation. 'He's going to kill you.'

'Yes, please,' said Sarah.

'What?' said Flower. 'You want to be killed?'

'No, I'm having mustard on my hot dog . . . eating always makes me feel better,' said Sarah.

'When you've had a door on your head?'

'I can't hear you, you're fading,' said Sarah.

In Flower's book of mobile etiquette this was always an excuse to get away. 'Stay on the line,' she said desperately, sounding like a police negotiator talking to a hostage taker and then she tried, 'Stop fucking pretending you're out of range,' but Sarah had gone. Flower set about texting her, very slowly, as she had learned neither text language nor speed on the keys and ended up doing laborious longhand. *Call me, let's sort things out.*

This text went mistakenly to Martha who texted back twenty minutes later *On my way*, too late for Flower to head her off and have a relaxing afternoon obsessively cleaning the flat or being cruel to animals, both of which were the special features of her PMT. Charlie and the cat cowered and Flower cleaned until there was a ring on the makeshift doorbell and Martha rolled in waving a scrappy bit of paper in front of her and announcing, 'We've got to crank things up a gear. I'm assuming you have something to report. Make me herbal tea and I'll kill you.' Then she flopped in a big pregnant heap on the mattress.

Flower explained Charlie's visit to Billy and Sarah, and Martha admired his courage mixed with extreme foolishness as she felt she could have predicted that poor Charlie might get floored by puffing Billy. She thought Charlie very sweet but a bit useless and decided that given the opportunity she wouldn't have any sort of sexual encounter with him.

Billy was different. In a strange echo of her mother's attraction to the brooding bad temper of Brian, there was something about Billy's sulkiness that fascinated Martha. She would melt down a drain if Sarah ever found this out though, as it was an unacknowledged cornerstone of their friendship that they would never sleep with each other's partners. Martha realised she was blushing and that

Flower was staring at her.

'Pah, hormones!' she said in an exaggerated fashion and tried to cover her face. Flower, used to hormonal explosions of her own as well as Martha's, didn't connect Martha's redness in any way with an assessment of the suitability of her and Sarah's partners for her bed.

Then the two friends sat down together and re-examined the list which contained the following elements:

Flower talk to him.

'Not much use,' said Flower. 'In fact, a bloody waste of time. I reckon it just made him feel more angry.'

'When did you do that?' said Charlie who, as usual, was eavesdropping.

'Oh, I just bumped into him in the newsagents,' said Flower.

'I thought you . . .' Martha said. Flower pinched the inside of Martha's arm really hard '. . . bumped into him in Sainsbury's.'

'For fuck's sake, girls,' said Charlie, 'does it really matter?'

Flower and Martha exchanged a look.

M talk to him.

'All right,' said Martha. 'I'll have a go.'

'Are you sure?' said Flower. 'You know he's getting worse.'

'Oh, I'll be all right,' said Martha. 'Surely he wouldn't whack a big pregger lady?'

'Yeah, you're right,' said Flower. 'Next?'

150

done, to last night's dinner. As Martha slogged furiously, feeling that this must be what it was like laying waste to rainforest as she chopped through the flat with a hoover and dustpan and brush, polish, duster and a sweet-smelling spray to squirt at anything that ponged, she had a strange sense of fear mixed with a tiny bit of deliciousness that Billy was going to be in her flat *alone with her* for at least a couple of hours.

Martha had not totally ignored the fact that she was going to give Billy a stiff talking to, but like many women, she truly believed that if Billy was with her, he wouldn't hit her. She pulled herself up when she realised that she was feeling too fond of Billy and kept telling herself that he was a violent person who hit her friend and therefore was not deserving of little thrills of anticipation.

Foolishly, given her pregnant state, Martha, then began to consume a six-pack of strong lager that she had found at the back of her wardrobe, obviously placed there at some time or other by a selfish party-goer who did not want to waste the alcohol content on a lesser man or woman. Martha thought she would have half a can to steady her nerves as she began to get the speech together in her head that she would give to Billy. As she hoovered, she slurped, and suddenly three cans had gone and she felt a bit drunk and a bit guilty. It was rather late in the day to get Lump pissed before she/he left the all-encompassing safety of her womb, but she was sure Lump could handle his/her booze. Martha could think of nothing nicer than floating pissed in a warm sea.

By early evening, she still had lots of clearing up to do, but unfortunately her enthusiasm for the job

155

had dribbled away with the fourth can, so she gathered up armfuls of rubbish and threw it all under her duvet: a cat tray, some pudding, a heap of dirty knickers, a cheap bottle of wine with the top not quite on, some leftover pizza and a home colonic irrigation kit. Just as the duvet floated over this bizarre collection of goods, there was a knock at the door. Martha got up to answer it, stumbled and realised she was quite pissed. I should be ashamed of myself, she thought, but I'm pissed so I won't bother.

'Hiya,' she said to no one in particular, well practised in disguising her pissedness, following many a Sunday dinner at home after a session in the pub. She felt warm and altruistic towards the world as she opened the door, although this leaked away when she saw how unsmiling Billy's face was. He had been in the local pub and was the worse for two barley wines, an uncommon drink these days, but which could be labelled the tipple of the unreconstructed psychopath, so often has it featured in scenarios in which some blokes go off to kick the shit out of some rival football fans, burgle an empty property or bring some woman to the point of tears.

'Come in,' urged Martha, trying hard to remember whether Billy would know she knew about the bathroom door incident. Of course he fucking well does, she said to herself, then realised she was slurring her unspoken words and swearing in her thoughts, which was a very bad sign.

Billy came in showing a remarkable degree of restraint at the sight of the recently tidied earthquake that was Martha's flat. For Martha, each can of extra-strong lager had given her flat

156

that gloss of neatness and a cachet which it simply didn't possess.

'Sit down,' she said, pointing to the kitchen table.

'Shall we just get started?' said Billy, looking at his watch. 'I've got quite a lot to do this evening. Where's your computer?'

Martha led him through to the room where the computer sat; the room was currently being occupied by Pat, who had decided to stay a few days but, because Martha had thought she would definitely screw things up if she was around, she had persuaded her mother to go to the West End and see a show. 'Seeing a show' was something that Pat's generation thought was a huge treat and she did not need much persuading, saying she would be back at eleven. Martha looked at her watch. It was 7.21 p.m. so she had almost four hours to get round to the topic of Billy's violence, have him lose his temper and retrieve the situation with her remarkable people skills before Pat got in. After half a lifetime Martha still didn't realise that she *had* no people skills.

Martha turned on her computer and Billy set about plugging bits in and clicking the mouse on a confusing array of icons at a remarkable speed. Martha felt too confused to ask him what he was doing. She had always had terrible trouble with electrics. Only last week, for example, a charming old West Indian guy like the universal grandfather of the world had come round and fixed her video for what seemed a laughably small fee and Martha had felt so grateful towards him she nearly cried.

'Can I try my handiwork?' he had asked and Martha had gestured at the pile of videos and said,

157

'Pick any one.'

As the picture spread onto the screen she realised that there in front of their eyes were two naked men one of whom was anally penetrating the other with gusto. 'It's an Italian art film,' she managed to get out as she observed the horrified look on the poor guy's face and thought to herself, Why did I even bother to say that?

The grandfather repair man left, sadly turning down her tip.

Billy seemed to be coming to the end of whatever complicated thing he was doing to her computer. He'd saved various files for her and the technical language swam past her like hieroglyphics made verbal as she nodded, pretending to understand. How to keep him there and talk about Sarah was now the problem.

'Can I get you a drink?' she said and was surprised when he looked enthusiastic about that idea. She found some vodka and scrubbed at a glass in the sink. Billy swigged it back in one, smiled and the evening seemed to begin.

Martha felt relaxed. Lump had drifted off to sleep inside her and chatting in a friendly fashion, she and Billy strolled into the lounge. Billy walked out onto the balcony and, in an extreme and by now predictable hormonal mood swing, an idea occurred to Martha in her drunkenness that she could throw him off the balcony and make it look like an accident. End result: a favour would have been done all round.

She began to estimate how much force she would need to run at him, and tip him over into the blackness of the South London night. She started to convince herself that this would work, and even

158

strolling. She wondered to herself why an alternative image of him drunkenly beating her hadn't surfaced ahead of the family group.

'No, better go,' he said.

Shall I ask him whether there'll be a repeat performance? thought Martha, briefly forgetting he was one of her best friend's boyfriends.

I hope she doesn't ask me if we're going to see each other again, thought Billy.

Just as Martha was about to humiliate herself by asking that very question, Pat quickly emerged from her room and holding out her hand said, 'How charming to meet you, and you are?'

'. . . Just going,' Billy managed to say and slid with an enormous sense of relief outside the front door.

'Seemed like a nice young man,' said Pat, as the door shut.

The phone rang. Unfortunately, Martha hadn't decided on her strategy yet so she coughed very loudly as her tearful friend left another message asking her to call.

Pat, whose hearing was very acute, had made out the gist of the message and looked sternly at her daughter.

'Oh dear, have you made love to a friend's fiancé?' she said.

Martha couldn't help herself, she laughed out loud at her mother's choice of words.

'Mum,' she said, 'I am in my late thirties and what I do is none of your business. I don't want to upset you, but you just have to accept that I am an adult and wrong as they may seem, I make my own choices.'

This would have been a perfectly acceptable

plea for independence had not a huge tear rolled down Martha's face, as she finished her little speech. Pat's stomach lurched as it always did when one of her little girls was upset and the two stood there with Martha crying as hard as she ever had and Pat trying to fold herself round her daughter's mountainous bump but not succeeding very well.

*   *   *

Sarah and Flower were in a café quite close to Martha's when they saw Billy walk past.

Sarah had phoned Flower in a panic when Billy didn't come home because it was the first time it had ever happened and Flower had gone over to keep her company until Charlie's phone calls got very frequent and she left about 2 a.m.

Sarah hadn't slept all night and Billy, who had started the night as someone who was beginning to irritate her slightly and with whom she might finish, not least because of the increasing violence, became by the morning a saintly and generous man whom she loved madly and who very occasionally was violent, probably because she goaded him into it.

Flower was not happy when she heard Sarah eulogising Billy as if he were St Francis of Assisi. It had crossed Flower's mind that Billy and Martha had spent the night together, but she didn't dare suggest it to Sarah, who was thinking it too, but wondered if it would be betraying her friend to even consider it. Flower had borne the brunt of Martha's hormonal outbursts during this pregnancy and therefore believed that any behaviour was possible.

164

'Billy!' screamed Sarah and ran out of the café.

Billy's heart missed a beat and his brain began to work overtime.

Sarah ran towards him as though he was a soldier come back from the war, but halfway across she remembered he had been out all night and skidded to a halt several inches from him.

'Where the fuck have you been?' was the unlyrical enquiry that escaped her lips.

Billy had decided to play it indignant and the plot his brain had delivered to him began to spray out.

'Look, Sarah, I'm sorry—I was round at Martha's and she felt really rough, thought the baby might be coming so we ended up going to Casualty and they took her in to see the doctor and I fell asleep in the waiting room and then Martha thought I'd gone home because she looked in the wrong place and they woke me up about seven this morning and I went and had some breakfast and now I've just been round to Martha's to see if it's all right. Christ, she's your friend—*you* should have been looking after her.'

'Sorry,' was Sarah's automatic response. Then she thought, Why am *I* saying sorry? He's the one who didn't contact me, and so she said this.

'I did. I bloody called you on your mobile,' bluffed Billy. 'Did you have it on all night?'

'Er . . .' Sarah began to falter. 'Why didn't you leave a message?'

'Well, I would have, but Martha was having a really bad spasm and I . . . well, I just got distracted. Most of the time I had it switched off in the hospital.'

'Then why didn't you call me later?'

165

' 'Cause I fucking fell asleep, for Christ's sake,' said Billy, managing to talk himself up to the moral high ground.

Flower, who was lurking in a gawky fashion in the background, didn't believe a word of it.

'Flower!' Suddenly Billy's voice burned her brain.

'Yes?' she answered.

'You believe me, don't you?'

'Yes,' said Flower and hated herself.

Sarah turned to her with an expression of semi-disbelief and appeal.

'I think he's telling the truth,' said Flower wanly.

'So, let's all go back to Martha's and see how she is,' said Sarah, looking for a flicker of guilt, panic or whatever.

'If you like,' Billy said casually, feeling relieved she couldn't see an EEG which would demonstrate the level of electrical activity in his brain: he could have run a power station on it. The three of them turned in a formation and headed down the road towards Martha's estate.

Martha nearly fainted when she opened the door to see the three of them. In the split second that followed, she assumed that Sarah hadn't pronounced her guilty of the worst betrayal of friendship because she hadn't hit her yet. But she had absolutely no idea what Billy had told the girls and therefore she waited for his lead. He, on the other hand, didn't want to make it too obvious by saying something like, 'Hi, how are you feeling after our trip to Casualty after you felt bad and I couldn't phone Sarah because of the emergency nature of the visit and then her mobile was turned off but anyway we thought that we'd pop round and see how you are.'

Instead he said, 'Feeling OK now?'

Sarah was watching them like a madwoman for signs of betrayal.

'Yes, much,' said Martha.

'Poor you,' said Flower, 'having to go there.'

Where does she mean? wondered Martha and took a lucky guess given her condition but just to be safe didn't mention the word.

'Yes, it was awful—noisy, dirty.'

'That's the NHS for you,' said Flower, confirming it for her.

Sarah was still glowering, trying to decide whether Martha looked like she'd been banged senseless all night or not.

Then Pat appeared out of the spare room. 'Hello everyone,' she said brightly.

Please, prayed Martha, don't let her give the game away. She turned towards her mother and made a panic-stricken face which Pat correctly interpreted as a clue that some sort of subterfuge was going on. Rather than put her foot in it she withdrew, making an excuse about having to wash her girdle.

Martha now had the floor and decided to trowel on the drama. 'I'm so grateful to Billy for taking me to Casualty and bearing with me,' she said. 'I felt bloody awful, like my insides were gradually being squeezed through my intestines to be shat out.'

'Yes, thank you, Martha,' said Flower, who was weedy about this sort of thing.

'Why didn't you call us?' said Sarah.

' 'Cause I was worried it had all gone wrong and I was going to lose the Lump and I just didn't know how I would react,' said Martha, and then felt incredibly guilty that she had used her unborn baby as an alibi for her unfaithfulness.

'Oh Martha, I'm really sorry,' said Sarah and Martha felt even worse because she realised that the corner had been turned and Sarah now believed that she and Billy had not done anything. She felt her eyes welling up with tears and realised that Billy was looking at her with contempt.

She just wished that everyone would piss off and leave her to get her head in gear and her story straight.

At that point Junior from next door popped his head round the balcony and said, 'Fucking hell, Martha, were you banging a bloody football team last night or what?'

A portentous silence followed.

CHAPTER TWENTY-ONE

Pat, without so much as a backward thought, stepped into the breach.

'It wasn't Martha, Junior,' she said. 'After all, she is nine months' pregnant. No, it was me. Embarrassed as I am to admit it, the Rev Brian was visiting and we got carried away.'

Junior felt physically sick at the thought of these two people of advancing years copulating noisily, not to mention wrinkly bits of skin flapping with wild abandon, forgetting that he possessed similar younger but equally wrinkly bits too and looked a bit silly himself when they were undulating furiously.

Flower also found herself disgusted at the

thought of Pat and the Rev, and then shovelled in some political correctness from somewhere to get her conscience back on an even keel. After all, she reasoned to herself, why shouldn't old people couple in any way they want? If they could cope with it, surely their younger relatives could turn a blind eye to the fact that they were being horribly carnal for their age.

Junior was seeing Martha's mum through new eyes. 'Oh, right you are then, Mrs Harris,' he said and slunk back to his balcony area to text all his friends and tell them what stomach-churning sexual practices were going on right under his nose.

Everybody shifted uncomfortably once Pat had made her revelations about her midnight shenanigans with the Rev Brian. Flower noticed that Billy had a little smirk on his face. Martha's expression was one Flower had never seen before nor was it intelligible as representing any recognisable emotion. Her nearest stab at it would have been an animal previously in great pain having been freed from a trap.

'Well, now we know Martha's all right perhaps we'd better go,' suggested Billy tentatively and everyone started to move towards the door. He and Sarah wished Martha and her mother an awkward goodbye and headed through the rubbish littering the walkway to play Lift Lottery, the game that is so popular on London's council estates.

Flower, who didn't want to catch them up, thereby giving them a chance to talk about the schism in their relationship thrown up by last night's absence, hung back. 'Can I just use your loo?' she said and headed off towards it wondering why she had asked and whether there is ever an occasion when access is denied by anybody. Surely it would be more sensible just to inform Martha she was off to use her toilet, but English manners forbade this as a faux pas more serious than urinating openly in a pot plant and Flower preferred to forget that particular birthday.

In the toilet Flower pondered the convincingness of Pat's statement and decided that it wasn't true and that she was covering up for Martha. But why would Martha do something as stupid as fucking Billy, especially when she knew what had been going on between him and Sarah? Before she had a chance to stop herself, Flower realised she was not just having a pee; something bigger, fashioned by obsessive consumption of bran was heading out, another huge catastrophe of etiquette and frowned upon by all but the most libertarian of toilet-owners. 'One should always shit in one's own toilet,' she mused to herself, pleased with her homespun homily but not really sure what it actually meant apart from what it literally meant.

Left alone for a couple of minutes, Martha said to Pat, 'Thanks a million for getting me out of trouble there, Mum.'

'I don't approve, Martha,' said Pat, 'but you're in enough trouble as it is,' throwing a glance at the Lump. 'Also,' she went on, 'I've decided to go back to your dad.'

'Mum, you can't,' said Martha. It was a pain having her there, but apart from her bedroom, which was out of bounds, the place was looking almost normal.

'It's my duty as a wife to be by your father's side, to love him, cherish him and do my best in the kitchen, at social events and between the sheets,'

other in. She only felt sorry that this session could not be shared with Sarah too.

'Oh Martha, I can't believe it. What happens when Sarah finds out?'

'She won't,' said Martha.

'Yes she will,' said Flower. 'You told me almost immediately. You'll crack within days.'

Martha knew she was right.

'And Billy's a violent man,' said Flower accusingly.

'Not with me he wasn't,' said Martha.

Flower realised she had been reduced to an 'Oh Martha,' machine as each new comment of Martha's brought out another sigh of despair.

'Anyway,' said Martha, 'I might kill him. I nearly did before I slept with him, you know.'

'Oh Martha,' Flower said automatically, then added, 'That is bullshit.'

'Honestly, Flower, it's not,' said Martha. 'These hormones flooding round your system make you want to do so many weird things. If I hadn't been so desperate for a fuck I'd never have jumped Billy.'

'Wouldn't Junior have done,' asked Flower, adding, 'if you were desperate?'

'What—and be had up before the beak for underage sex?' said Martha. 'No, ta.' Then she stopped talking for a while and just stared.

'Are you OK?' said Flower.

Martha wasn't. She felt warm all round her thigh area and realised that her waters were breaking. It seemed, for a second, like a big warm sea swirling round her and she stood up helplessly as she tried to work out how much of what felt like a tributary had flowed down the main gangway of the wine

175

bar.

There was quite a lot.

Flower saw it and thought Martha had wet herself, and much to her shame was logging it away in the area of her brain that memorised things her friends did which could be worked into a comedy routine.

The half-dead barman, bearing something enormous on a plate that Martha had ordered, stepped unsuspectingly onto the skidpan created by her amniotic fluids and slid almost gracefully towards the bar before he fell, bruising his coccyx very badly in the process.

'Quick, call an ambulance!' shouted Flower and the sleepy bar sprang into life.

Within minutes an ambulance sped up and two paramedics scooped up the beleaguered barman, leaving Flower and Martha to run along behind protesting that they needed an ambulance too.

CHAPTER TWENTY-TWO

The staff at the local Accident and Emergency weren't particularly impressed by Martha and seemed far more keen to move the half-dead barman into a cubicle for treatment. To Martha it was the most momentous time of her life, whereas to the A and E staff, another cursory welcome into the world of a squealing mass of redness was about as dull as it got.

'But my water has burst,' shouted Martha at the disappearing arse of a very officious, obviously sexually frustrated and childless staff nurse.

She turned and said, '*Its* waters have broken actually, and I suggest you just go home and wait for the contractions.'

Martha, who had based her knowledge of pregnancy and birth on Hollywood films and adverts rather than actual textbooks, which she kept meaning to get round to reading, but just hadn't, turned dejectedly to Flower and suggested they went home.

Flower nodded and got her special emergency tenner out from her mobile phone case to pay for a cab as she felt the situation demanded it. Her phone had been turned off in the hospital and when she turned it back on, it rang immediately telling her she had six new messages, all from Charlie, of course, the next more urgent and louder than the one before and seeming to convey that some injury had occurred during the demo and that he was off to get some treatment.

So while the cab driver gave Martha a rundown on the births of his six children, Flower called Charlie.

'Shit,' he said in reply to her enquiry about how he was, followed by his description of the trajectory of the policeman's boot.

'So just how far up your arse did it go?' enquired Flower, oblivious to the fact that the cab driver, a confirmed homophobic, was getting completely the wrong idea.

Martha gave her a look after which point she became barely audible at the other end of the phone and Charlie assumed she was in a bad reception area and hung up.

Contractions started even before the cab had reached its destination and Martha wondered

177

whether they should turn right round again and head for the hospital but Flower vaguely remembered that you should wait for a few hours, until as she put it rather unscientifically, 'They're really fucking killing you,' before you ventured off to hospital.

'Should you go and minister to poor Charlie?' said Martha, silently praying, an odd thing for the wayward daughter of a vicar to do, that Flower would stay with her.

Flower was so used by now to Charlie's encounters with the constabulary and his resulting injuries that she promised she would stay for the day and keep an eye and then accompany Martha into hospital.

So what do you do on a day when your Lump is about to become a real baby?

Martha felt she should do something dramatic and memorable. Flower suggested in that case she might want to have a stab at cleaning her bedroom, and strangely enough, as is often noted with the late stage of pregnancy, a nesting instinct overtook Martha and she swooped into her bedroom and began a major clear-up of evidence from her liaison the night before, coupled with the removal of grime of months. After several hours and increasing pain, she had created quite a nice little haven for her and Lump to exist in for the first few weeks of Lump's life.

By early evening the frequency of contractions had increased enough for Martha to ring the hospital, having glanced at her book of what to do if you're having a baby, and tell them she thought labour was imminent.

The hospital agreed and Martha asked when the

'Well, I was in London for a conf—' he began, when Pat cut him off and said, 'Come on, Martha, did you really think we wouldn't come to celebrate the birth of our daughter's first child?'

Martha felt that now would be a good time to express some of the feelings she'd been suppressing for years, under the guise of the Just Given Birth Hormone coursing through her body and making her uncontrollably honest. She could visualise Pat explaining this to her father as he fumed in the car on the way home. This was one encounter she *wasn't* going to lose out on, and perhaps the fact that her best friends were there to witness it wasn't such a bad thing. She motioned to people to sit on the few weedy chairs that were around and marvelled at the fact that somehow she had ended up in a private room. She wasn't sure why; it could have been her threats to the midwife that went on after the baby was born—threats which are supposed to stop once labour is ended but in Martha's case became louder in volume and more unpleasant.

'So what are you going to call it?' sneered her father and it was the sneering that was responsible for Martha's reply.

'Jesus,' she said.

Rev Brian looked aghast and Pat looked equally shocked by proxy. There was some giggling too. Greasy Ted threw his head back and roared with laughter and Sarah just continued to look pissed off and stare at the floor.

'That is sacrilege!' bellowed Rev Brian. 'I'll give you twenty-four hours to think about it, and after that time if you persist with this pathetic idea I will never speak to you or see you again.'

185

He exited with as much melodrama as he could muster, with Pat in tow talking all the time in a low voice and trying to calm him down, not realising that over the years it never failed to wind him up even more.

Two down and a mere five to go, thought Martha and decided to apply her truth-telling hormonality to the others in the room. 'Ted, why are *you* here?' she said. Ted appeared from behind a big bunch of flowers. From such beauty, ugliness comes shining through, thought Martha and wondered if that was a famous quote or just her own effort.

'Well, as your employer,' said Ted, 'I happened to phone Sarah and ask her how you were getting on and she'd just heard from Flower about the baby so I thought I'd better pop down and see how you were and give you congratulations.' He sounded stilted, less funny and less relaxed in this setting.

'Just as well you did,' said Martha, 'because it's your baby.'

There was a look of such tragic proportions on Ted's face that she thought he might hit her. Instead he said, 'You fucking cow, Martha,' threw the flowers on the floor and walked out of the room. Martha noted that she felt really upset, but how could she tell if it was genuine?

'You idiot,' said Flower. 'What did you do that for?'

Martha felt slightly ashamed so she went on the offensive. 'Oh, mind your own business, you flaky hippy and leave me in peace—and take *him* with you.' She pointed to Charlie.

Flower was knackered and grumpy, and didn't

need a second invitation. She grabbed Charlie by the hand and almost lifted him off the ground they left so fast. Martha felt like a spectator at her own funeral.

Just then, Martha's mobile phone rang. She picked it up, looked at the caller display, pressed the answer button and just said, 'Fuck off.' Then she turned back to the remnants of the baby-welcoming party, Sarah with her black eye and Billy shuffling uncomfortably from foot to foot.

Martha sighed, then opened her mouth and said to Sarah, 'Another black eye, I see. No need to wonder where *that* came from. Well, if him hitting you won't make you leave him, perhaps this will . . .' She didn't finish the sentence because a stinging slap caught her on the side of the face.

It was Billy.

'You're hysterical,' he said. 'We'll come back when you're feeling better. Come on, Sarah.' He led her from the room.

'That went well,' said stern midwife, coming out of the ensuite toilet.

'Just get me my morphine,' shouted Martha, who believed if a Class A drug was written up for you legally, you might as well take full advantage of it.

Martha pondered the enormity of what she had done while Jesus slept. She only had to hold out twenty-four hours and her father would never speak to her again. Oh, what bliss. She didn't know what to do about Ted, about whom she felt rather regretful, and as for her outburst to Flower—that was completely ridiculous: she had no axe to grind there at all. And Flower had been a tower of strength. Poor Sarah, her intervention couldn't have been more textbook stupid.

187

I must sort everything out when I leave here, thought Martha, suddenly grateful for a few moments' peace. Little did she realise that with a baby in tow, finding the time to sort things out was about as likely as her father reappearing at the door and saying, 'Fuck it, love, why not have another one and call it God?'

There was a knock on the door. Oh Christ, who is it now? thought Martha. 'Yes?' she shouted grumpily.

Junior opened the door and slunk into the room. He had a hunted look about him and the reason for this was revealed soon enough when he was followed in by his mum and two policemen. Jesus, in a worryingly anti-authority response to their arrival, woke up and started to cry very loudly.

'Will you explain to them, Martha,' said Junior. 'They don't believe my story about the BMW.'

'I'm sorry,' said Martha, looking blankly at him, 'I don't know who you are.'

A smile spread over the face of the younger copper.

'Only kidding,' said Martha and turned to Junior's mum. 'Look, I'm really sorry, Mrs Shakespeare,' she said. 'I know I shouldn't be encouraging him into bad habits . . . it was an emergency.'

'So I see,' said Junior's mum, picking up Jesus and asking, 'What's he called?'

'Haven't decided yet,' said Martha, wondering for the first of many times whether she could go through with the Jesus thing, especially given there were so many fundamentalist churches in her area. Jesus quietened down as soon as Mrs Shakespeare picked him up and Martha felt rather jealous.

188

'Oh, he's absolutely gorgeous,' she said. 'His daddy must be really pleased.'

'Hmmm,' said Martha.

The older policeman coughed in an attention-seeking sort of way.

'Yes, finish your business,' said Martha, 'and then please get out of my room.'

'Can I ask you a couple of questions, madam?' he said.

'Look,' said Martha, 'I'll tell you exactly what happened. I was about to have a baby and I didn't want to go to hospital on the bus. Call me a snob if you want, I had no money for a cab and so Junior very helpfully got a car for us to get there quickly and safely. I'm sorry he stole it.'

Junior nodded solemnly.

'Well, I suppose that puts a marginally different complexion on things,' said the senior policeman, looking like he had enjoyed saying 'marginally'. His colleague nodded.

'We'll be in touch, son,' said the older one.

They left leaving an awkward Junior and his mum by the bed looking around as if they had never seen a hospital room before. Junior's mum suddenly stirred.

'We'd better go too,' she said. She turned to Martha. 'Look, girl,' she said, 'is the father around?'

'I'm not really sure,' said Martha. 'I should have a better idea by the end of the week.'

'Well,' said Mrs Shakespeare, 'if you need any advice on coping with the little lad, let me know, or I'll babysit or whatever.'

'Thank you,' said Martha. 'I'd be grateful of that sometime, I'm sure.'

Suddenly she was alone.

'But I'm not alone, though,' she said out loud.

'No, you're not alone,' said stern midwife, coming into the room with some tablets for her.

'You're right, Jesus is with me,' said Martha, evoking a rather strange look from stern midwife. If she did plump for 'Jesus', Martha could tell there were going to be many moments like this when people would think she was a Christian of the over-committed variety. As for poor Jesus himself, how would he cope in the playground? Would he be bullied, laughed at, maybe worshipped—who could tell?

Martha could still extricate herself from the 'Jesus' commitment. Only a small roomful of people had heard her pronouncement and she would lose no face by saying she'd decided to change the name of her baby to Wilson or Brad or one of those fashionable surname-type names that every poor little bastard in South London had been saddled with. Why not Harris? Harris Harris, there was a name to contend with.

She was pondering this question when Jesus/Harris began to cry and stern midwife suggested she feed him as Martha was too knocked off to come up with that obvious solution to his distress. Up until this point her attempts at breastfeeding had been singularly unsuccessful but it now felt like things were reaching a crisis point and Jesus's cries rang louder and louder round the room, giving rise to awful dark fantasies in Martha's mind that she wouldn't be able to feed him and the poor little guy would just fade away to nothing.

'I killed Jesus,' she said to herself.

and he disappeared into the bedroom, reappearing within seconds with a smile on his face, saying, 'Here we are. Send her my love, won't you?' as though Sarah was just going on a long weekend with the girls rather than having been thrown round her own flat by him, causing her to run away.

Flower stood still for a very long time, trying desperately to decide on a course of action.

'Anything else?' said Billy, who had decided at all costs not to ask Flower to beg Sarah to come back to him, and had vowed not to threaten any of Sarah's friends. He was so charming that Flower, to her complete shame, found herself fleetingly wondering if Sarah was exaggerating it.

Billy coughed. 'Is Martha well?' he enquired, as if pushed to make polite conversation.

'Fine,' said Flower and thought, I can hardly wave a fucking gun around and tell him to watch it now.

'Right then,' she said. 'I'd better be going. Shall I give Sarah a message?'

'You can say I know we both let it get a bit heated,' said Billy, 'and I for one am very sorry.'

'OK,' said Flower hesitantly. 'See you then.'

*   *   *

Suddenly she was on her bike and on the way home, the video of the incident in her head having been completely erased by the reality. She called Charlie. 'Yeh fine,' she said into her mobile. 'See you in ten minutes.'

Then she called Martha. 'Couldn't fucking do it.'

'Thank Christ,' said Martha. 'Hoped you'd come to your senses.'

'Oh thanks,' said Flower. 'Cheers. Oh, by the way,' she added, 'saw your dad in the pub and did a terrible thing. Told him you weren't calling Jesus, Jesus. I think he might come round.'

'He's already here,' said Martha.

'Oh, right you are. I'll be off. What are you going to call him then?' she added, almost as an afterthought.

'Got to go,' said Martha annoyingly. 'Talk to you later.'

'I've got a gig at the—' started Flower then realised she was talking to air.

* * *

Martha's dad was indeed sitting there looking marginally less grumpy than usual. He had called Pat from a phone box to tell her the good news and Pat had been so relieved, having felt awful about just trotting after him at the hospital.

'So, what are you going to call him?' said the Rev.

They had all reached this point because the Rev had arrived in the middle of a screaming row about the name. Flower had really landed them in it, having to come up with a name on the spot. Ted wanted to call the baby Melvin after his father but Martha told him that no way was any child of hers going to have a sex-offender's name. She herself wanted to call him Jude—at which Ted remarked that his son wasn't going to have a girl's name. A furious, noisy statemate had been reached, coinciding with the Reverend's arrival. The Rev Brian stood grinning on the doorstep, thinking to himself what a relief it was to finally hear someone

Sarah braced herself as Sim began. 'In the land of Tasmania, good and evil had fought a constant battle over thousands of years. The good people of Tasmania lived together in harmony on the mountain while the low, hairy, vile people of the plains lurked at the forest edge, carrying off the occasional good person's daughter to ravish and take into slavery.

'One day the good people realised they only had one beautiful daughter left, the daughter of the chief, and they resolved, much as they hated fighting, to defend her to the last life. Sure enough the low hairy people ('Was Charlie one of them?' Sarah wanted to ask) crept to the village in the middle of the night and snatched the chief's beautiful daughter. The good people sprang from their beds and a great battle commenced until sure enough all the good people lay dead or dying and the chief of the low people carried away the sobbing daughter of the good chief. A tear fell on his neck as they ran and he changed in an instant into a snake and slithered away and that is how the Tasmanian Devil was born.'

Sim sat back with a smug look on his face.

'Hang on a sec,' said Charlie. 'The Tasmanian Devil's not a snake.'

'Whatever,' said Sim.

'Yeh, whatever,' said Charlie and handed Sarah a freshly rolled joint.

Sarah took a massive pull on it and nearly catapulted back through the wall.

'Christ Almighty, Flower,' she said hoarsely, 'that is some fucking blow, man.'

Flower, who was inured to its power and quite stoned, nodded absentmindedly and didn't think to

243

try and contain this novice's intake. Sarah went remarkably quiet for about half an hour and when Flower asked her if she wanted herb tea, Sarah looked at her with an expression of pure malice and said, 'I am evil.'

'Oh dear,' said Flower, 'the double zero's got her.'

'Right,' said Sim, 'here's another really cool tale from Tasmania called "Why the Trees Don't Talk Any More".'

'I'm not Sarah any more,' said Sarah.

'Hey, chill babe,' said Sim. 'There might be something in this story for you.'

'Only my death would be any relief,' said Sarah.

'Fucking hell,' said Sim, looking worriedly at Flower and Charlie. ' 'Fraid I can't oblige you there, little princess.'

Then Sim, never one to be too concerned by the mental state of his audience—for if he had, he wouldn't have had an audience—ploughed on regardless.

'In Tasmania,' he said, 'the trees used to talk to each other, man.'

Sarah began to cry.

'Yeh, I know it's beautiful, babe,' he said.

Sarah snarled like a wolf and this sent an alarm signal to Flower who was pretty stoned so it was as if the cry for help came down a very long cottonwool tunnel. Then Sarah began to howl.

'Yeh, carry on, delightful lady,' said Sim, 'there was wolves on this island. Glad you're joining in. Anyway, to continue the story,' he said, 'the trees would make love with words and their green branches would swoosh with anticipation . . .'

'You want a story?' said Sarah. 'Here's one for

244

you, you boring hippy twat. It's the story of a little girl born into the shitty world of an ex-prostitute who was knocked up by a client and got her dates wrong, so missed out on having a legal abortion by two weeks. The illegal one failed so the baby arrived into a nasty little flat in an evil town and the order of the day for that little girl was to shut the fuck up while Mum's at work so the neighbours don't ring the social. A selection of boyfriends passed through: some of them hit the girl, some of them touched her up and some of them, she had to suck off.'

Sim looked bemused and Flower and Charlie's middle-class sensitivity showed on their faces.

'Sarah,' said Flower gently, 'you don't have to do this.'

Sarah ignored her. '. . . And then when she grew up the girl got away and met someone really handsome and intelligent and breathed a sigh of relief, until one day he hit her . . .' Sarah buried her head in her hands and began to sob.

'So what poor slag's that about?' said the ever-prescient Sim.

For once Charlie was puncher not punchee.

Sim was reluctantly ushered out of the door protesting that his best story so far from Zimbabwe about the witchdoctor's chickens, had been left unaired.

Flower lay Sarah down on the makeshift bed, put a blanket over her and hoped she'd have a good night free of demons.

*　　　*　　　*

In the morning the flat looked immaculate; the

dope had obviously had a bit of an odd effect as Sarah had cleaned it from top to bottom, dropping unconscious at about six o'clock in the morning.

'I took an aspirin for my headache,' she explained and Charlie kept quiet.

No one had done anything sensible like check the weather for the demo, so Sarah's wailing 'I don't know what to wear,' made Flower even more irritable than she already was.

'It's not like a party or a wedding,' she told her. 'You can wear what you like—express yourself through colours and fabrics.'

'But I like to be told what to wear, so I know,' said Sarah, whose lack of structure and security as a child ensured she now imposed a rigid routine on all her domestic chores and a system of coding her clothes that would defeat the most anal of obsessive compulsives. In the end Flower chose the least formal things she could find in Sarah's suitcase, all of which had been painfully pressed and folded.

'Will I need an umbrella?' said Sarah.

'Only to thump a pig with,' said Charlie cheerfully.

'Are there going to be animals there, then?' said Sarah. Charlie gave up and decided to leave well alone in Sarah's mind which to him seemed to be a vacuum with the odd bit of celebrity knowledge floating about in it.

Sarah, Flower and Charlie caught a bus up to the City to the prearranged meeting place. The atmosphere was relaxed and unthreatening although Charlie immediately pinpointed the troublemakers who would doubtless produce some medieval instrument of torture from their rucksacks and continuously bang it on the heads of policemen until they flew off.

The demo was at the vague behest of an umbrella organisation which covered a loose federation of eco-friendly groups brought together by the internet and with their main aim to destroy global capitalism. Unfortunately, no one in any of the organisations had worked out how this could be done properly so the groups were forced to gather at centres of global capitalism like the City of London where they were today and shout abuse in the vain hope that all the City boys on the dealing floors would suddenly see sense, stop washing for a bit and join their ranks and curtail their evil operations. Except it was a Saturday and the place was deserted bar protesters and police.

There was music, a few stalls selling food, lots of singing and dancing, and for once Sarah felt attracted to this world she had looked at from the sidelines for the past week.

'So it's not just dirty dogs on a rope, is it?' she said to Flower.

'No, it's not,' said Flower, who felt under pressure for some reason she couldn't put her finger on.

Sarah had assumed that as Flower was trying to be a comedian she would be funny all the time at home but was shocked to discover the opposite: Flower was akin to a pressure cooker, letting out little bits of steam here and there and often on the point of exploding. Sarah knew all about Flower's legendary PMT and why Charlie didn't have a dog which he had always wanted. Flower had explained that she would only kick it every month when she was stressed, and when Charlie looked at the way

247

Flower treated *him* monthly, he was pleased they didn't have a dog as its poor arse would by now be concave.

Charlie and Flower were chatting when Sarah said, 'Hey, isn't that Martha and Ted coming with, er, what is he called?'

'Don't know,' said Flower. 'Hey, Martha!'

Martha had seen something about the demo on the local news and felt sure Charlie and Flower would go along, taking poor Sarah with them. It would be an opportunity to tell them Jesus's new name. Ted agreed, but was along on sufferance and once he saw the array of raggle-taggle hippies everywhere, part of him, and he put it down to his age, felt rather sorry for the minibuses of young policemen spotty and raw who sat waiting for crusty Armageddon.

Martha, Sarah and Flower all kissed and hugged, because this was the first time for a while that they had all been together. The place was starting to get more crowded and bustling so the naming ritual had to be done while there was still room and they could all hear. Martha got the baby out of his buggy and held him up like a trophy, which he didn't much like and started to grizzle.

'As you know, everyone, we couldn't agree on a name,' said Martha. 'I wanted Jude, Ted wanted Melvin after his dad. So we've decided to compromise and we would like you to meet . . .' there was a short pause '. . . Jelvin!'

This was followed by a long silence in which the entire population of the demo seemed to stand in openmouthed horror.

Bloody hell, that's worse than Jesus, thought Sarah.

248

'Only kidding,' said Ted. 'It's John.'

A sigh of relief spread over the group. Flower was still worried Martha might have done something stupid, like given John the middle name of 'The Baptist', but no, it was just good old John. Nobody had broached the fact yet that Ted ran a lap-dancing club and Flower wondered whether she should mention it.

'What do you think?' she asked Sarah. 'Should I say something to clear the air?'

'What, you mean ask him for a job?' said Sarah. 'I might do too, I'm bored shitless in that call centre.'

Flower stared into the chasm that was the gap between her and Sarah socially, culturally and, well, in every way.

'No, I didn't mean that, Sarah. I meant how unacceptable it is as far as women are concerned for these clubs to exist.'

'Oh, lighten up,' said Sarah. 'People don't care about that sort of shit any more.'

Perhaps they don't care about domestic violence any more, either, thought Flower but said, 'Well, they bloody should and I'm sick of it.'

'Oi grumpy,' said Sarah.

'Sorry,' said Flower. 'Forget it.' And she kept her mouth shut, because she didn't want to get into a row with Ted on today of all days, a lovely sunny one with a happy band of protesters.

Unfortunately this didn't last long.

As the group stood round chatting, a missile hit Flower on the back of the head, 'missile' being the euphemism used in these scenarios for anything bigger and heavier than a bar of chocolate.

'Ow,' said Flower and looked down to see what

the missile was. It was a quarter of a brick and she marvelled that it hadn't knocked her out. It seemed to have come from the area where the police were.

'The police have started something!' she screamed at Charlie above the music.

'Right,' said Charlie, 'they're not getting away with this,' and he pushed his way through the crowd towards the straggly police line, as were many other men dressed in exactly the same uniform as Charlie.

'Don't do anything stupid,' shouted Flower at Charlie's retreating back, which was a bit like shouting after a cat, 'Leave those mice alone, now won't you.'

Ted suddenly realised that his baby and Martha were in the middle of a riot just about to go off and he said to Martha, 'We'd better get going,'

Martha, temporarily forgetting that she had given birth a few days ago, was quite keen to get stuck in, calling him a spoilsport.

'Come on, let's go,' said Ted.

It was too late. The unrest had spread quickly and there was no way out as the police had surrounded what they thought was the biggest group of troublemakers and, like sheepdogs herding sheep, were trying to force them down a side street where they could control them better, rough them up a bit and drag out the ringleaders.

Martha saw a few people attack McDonald's. 'Look at those stupid bastards,' she said, 'and I'm bloody starving.'

'They're fighting the influence of global capitalism,' said Flower.

'Well, standards have dropped in there recently. Maybe they need a wakeup call,' said Sarah.

'Come on, Martha,' said Ted, and tried to push the opposite way to the crowd; as he was such a big bloke, it started to work. Martha, John, Flower and Sarah trailed in his wake and after much shoving and cursing, with their nostrils assailed by unwashedness and hippy perfume, they reached the edge.

'Let me out, mate,' said Ted to a copper on the edge. 'I've got my family here and I'm worried they'll get hurt.'

'Should have thought of that before you joined the troublemakers,' said the policeman. 'Stay where you are.'

'Oh come on,' said Ted. 'We're caught up in this totally innocently.'

'Let us out please,' said Martha. 'I'm dying for a pee and I feel faint.'

'Shut it, slag,' said the copper.

This was too much for Ted and with his clenched fist propelled at some speed, the policeman was soon sprawled on the ground with no helmet, looking very angry.

CHAPTER THIRTY

Ted was immediately swarmed over by a group of policemen on a mission, the mission being to uphold the honour of their colleague who had, rather too easily some felt, plummeted to the deck at the lightest of touches. Still, however hard Ted's touch had been it didn't matter because one by one they took it in turns to kick him.

Martha was overcome with shock by this

behaviour being practised so openly. Rather naively she had imagined that, at the very least, the police would make an effort to pretend they weren't a bunch of thugs, but they didn't seem too bothered.

At one point, as blows were flailing down upon him, Ted received a few curt words in his ear to the effect that he was under arrest and would be taken down to the police station and dealt with. Ted sighed, aware that his arrival at that particular venue would probably involve another flurry of blows from Her Majesty's finest.

Martha tried bravely to reason with the policemen who had arrested Ted but as they weren't the sort of men who would support the idea of paternity leave and this was Martha's starting point, it seemed highly unlikely they would let Ted go home on the basis of being the father of a newborn baby.

Sarah amazingly found herself outraged, too. Given that she had lived her life in a right-wing tabloid cocoon of sanctimony, she had, up until now, refused to admit that bad police behaviour existed. As for more subtle concepts, like class differences, a little clock ticking in her head had started to count down to enlightenment. Billy's words rang in her ears, the putdowns, the swearing, the threats—and suddenly she saw him as a very successful policeman. Perhaps she should suggest a career-change. He might hit others instead of her. She joined in Martha's pleading to no avail and found herself addressing the big policeman as 'a cunt', not something he liked to be called and certainly a word Sarah would never have imagined herself using a week or so ago, particularly to a policeman.

'Well done,' said Martha, patting her on the back and temporarily forgetting that her man was buried underneath a sea of serge and about to be removed.

Suddenly the police sprang into action, lifted Ted up as though he was a great big coffin and ran with him to a van and delivered him into the back as though he was a big sack of shit in a great big coffin.

Martha, whose hormones were continuing to race around her body at almost the same rate as they had when she gave birth, burst into tears as Flower ineffectually shouted, 'Die, you pigs,' to the backs of the policemen and Sarah joined in sounding awkward but with a fair degree of gusto.

Suddenly Charlie appeared from nowhere licking an iced lolly as if he was on a day out at the seaside. Everyone looked at him aghast and he returned their look with a benign perplexed face.

'What?' said Charlie, and then he realised that Martha was crying, Sarah was redfaced and looked like she wanted a fight and Flower had her usual demonstration expression on, a mixture of bemusement and aggression.

'For Christ's sake, Charlie,' she said irritatedly. 'You've missed everything. They've taken Ted away.'

'That proto-fascist,' said Charlie. 'What did he do? Beat up a woman?'

Martha stopped crying. 'Fuck off, Charlie,' she said. 'He may not have your Glastonbury credentials but at heart he's a decent man.'

'Tell that to the junkie women with AIDS he employs in his lap-dancing club,' said Charlie.

'Oh grow up,' said Martha. 'They're all posh students raking in a fucking fortune.'

'They're exploited, man,' said Charlie.

John started to cry.

'Right, I'm off,' said Martha. 'Suppose I'd better find out what's happening with Ted.'

'I'll come with you,' said Sarah. 'I might talk to you about getting a job with Ted.'

'Sarah,' said Flower, 'what the hell are you thinking of?'

'Well, I've got the figure,' said Sarah, 'and I bet it's a fuck of a sight better than my present shitty job. Anyway, do I always have to have a politically cracked reason for you?'

'It's "correct",' said Flower.

'What will Billy say?' said Martha, before she could stop herself.

'I don't care,' said Sarah. 'Billy and I aren't together any more.'

Flower and Martha clapped and danced up and down on the spot. Charlie looked pleased too.

'Come on then,' said Martha to Sarah and off they went.

Flower and Charlie watched them go and the crowd seemed to part for them. Charlie shook his head. 'Should we talk her out of it?' he said, unthinkingly lighting a joint.

'Nah,' said Flower. 'I don't think you could.'

Just then, a policeman flew almost horizontally through the air at Charlie, rugby-tackling him to the ground. And that was how Charlie and Ted ended up sharing a rather small cell at the local police station.

* * *

The cell was packed. It contained two pickpockets who'd taken advantage of the crowds to see what they could drum up, a mentally ill hippy whose care in the community wasn't being managed very well, since he tended to drift towards any trouble that was going on, a man who had hit his girlfriend during an argument, and two teenage boys who had stolen a car and driven it round the fringes of the demo aiming an air rifle at anyone they didn't like the look of. Charlie and Ted got themselves into a corner and tried to avoid any involvement with the madness going on around them.

As there wasn't much else to do, Charlie cast himself in the role of the father of the bride, interviewing Ted as to his suitability as Martha's partner. It was natural that Charlie should launch straight into the subject of the club that Ted ran, as he had spent so much of his life railing against this industry that he felt it his duty to try and take it apart brick by metaphorical brick.

'Women are just treated like objects, man,' opined Charlie, 'and you're encouraging that.'

'Look mate,' said Ted, exasperated and bruised and unfamiliar with the inside of a cell, 'I'm not arguing with you and yes, that's the way our society is, but isn't it better that if these places have to exist, that they are run by someone like me who's kind to the girls and makes sure they're safe.'

'So you don't perv them up then?' asked Charlie.

'No, I don't "perv them up" as you so charmingly put it,' said Ted. 'Come down one night and see.'

'Flower would never allow it,' said Charlie, with a very slight trace of regret.

'Bring Flower too,' said Ted.

255

Charlie guffawed loudly at this suggestion and imagined himself asking Flower, particularly when she had PMT. He shuddered.

'Has someone just walked over your grave?' said Ted.

'No, but they fucking would do if I ever asked them down a lap-dancing club,' said Charlie.

Ted laughed. 'I'll have a word with her,' he said.

'I hope they let us out by tonight,' said Charlie. 'Flower's got a gig in Maidstone, and it's her last one before she does her first proper night at London's top comedy club tomorrow. I really want to go and support her.'

'You'll be lucky,' said Ted. 'I reckon we're due a night in the cells.'

Charlie realised that being with big ugly Ted was protecting him, the puny scruffy old hippy, and for the first time in ages, he felt quite secure. Ted only had to look at the other guys in the room to warn them off and his great big body acted as a solid reassuring barrier during the night.

*   *   *

Flower and Martha had tracked Charlie and Ted down to the same police station on Flower's mobile and were told they would probably be released sometime in the morning when they had been processed.

They're not lumps of cheese, thought Flower to herself, and was then reminded of Charlie's old sandals that she could not persuade him to throw away.

'Shit,' she said aloud. 'We'll have to go to Maidstone on our own.'

'Oh yes, I'll be fine,' said Sarah. 'I'll get as near the front as I can and cheer my head off. Don't worry it'll be great.'

'I hope so,' said Flower, wishing that they had the third member of their threesome there to bolster her confidence and shout abuse at any potential hecklers.

She made her way round the back to the makeshift dressing-room, a smallish box in which a couple of foldable chairs and a broken mirror on a ratchety table were the only concessions to showbusiness.

In the room were Mal Fogarty, the compère, a local guy who worked at the abattoir and whose scary Northern wife Glenys wouldn't let him go to comedy gigs very often, partly because it was 'a load of fookin' shite' but mainly because she was frightened that he'd give up his fulltime job and end up earning a pittance and then fail, leaving them all on the dole. Tonight, however, because he was near home, his wife had sanctioned his regular compèring slot and she was secretly delighted with the seventy quid he brought home every week, proudly telling anyone at work who'd listen that her husband was a stand-up comic.

Two other comics had travelled down from London, one of them called Terry Twat and the other, Jake Ashkenazy. Both were totally different in style, Terry Twat emphasising his speech impediment and falling over a lot, whereas Jake Ashkenazy had a rather serious and clever political act which he feared would not be best suited to the good burghers of Maidstone. Unfortunately, it hadn't been best suited to the good burghers of anywhere—apart from a political benefit he had done to a group of seriously committed activists who had all but carried him out on their shoulders whilst wetting themselves with joy after his twenty-minute exposition on the recent troubles in the Middle East.

Flower had met Terry Twat, real name Joe Evans, on a number of occasions and always found him to be a nice bloke who was good fun, whereas Jake was rather distant and somewhat superior, a trait displayed by many left-wing comics whose socialist credentials don't quite extend to treating their fellow man with much respect. Jake was incredibly posh, which seemed strange to Flower, as he had eschewed all that to live on an estate in North London, and although a big part of her admired him for this, she also thought it made him a wanker as well. It was interesting to see him in a room with a real member of the working-class like Mal because Jake didn't have a lot to say to him apart from seeming embarrassed to be in his company. Terry Twat chatted away easily and asked Flower how her comedy life was going.

'Not too bad,' said Flower, her stomach churning at the prospect of the night's proceedings. 'I've got my first gig tomorrow at the Comedy Store, but I've had this odd heckler wandering around at my gigs and just fucking things up for me.'

'What, like a stalker?' said Jake.

'I wouldn't quite say that,' said Flower, 'but he's appeared more times than I feel comfortable with.'

'I'm surprised Charlie's not here tonight,' said Terry. 'I would have thought he'd want to protect you.'

'He's in prison,' said Flower, 'for causing some trouble at a demo.'

Jake Ashkenazy visibly perked up. 'Oh, do tell me he hit a fucking fascist, darling girl,' he said.

'No, he was caught smoking a joint,' said Flower. 'I'm sure they'll let him out soon.'

'Wow,' said Jake. 'Was he at the demo earlier today?'

'Yes,' said Flower. 'So was I.'

'Fucking great, wasn't it?' said Jake. 'We showed those pigs a thing or two. I got a couple of digs in at them.'

'You twatted a copper?' said Mal.

Jake noticed that the muscles on Mal's neck were slightly strained and his face had taken on a bull-like quality that wasn't there before he mentioned hitting a policeman. He backtracked and laughed in an embarrassed fashion.

'Not really hit him, man,' he said. 'Shouted at him—you know.'

'Well, I hope you didn't hit a copper, because I might have to hit *you*,' said Mal.

Jake quivered and looked at the floor. Mal winked at Flower. The landlord stuck his head round the door. 'I think we're ready, mate,' he told Mal. 'The natives are getting restless.'

'Right you are,' said Mal.

It had been decided that Jake would go on first, Flower in the middle and Terry Twat at the end to balance the show properly. Flower wished she could go on first, so there was a good excuse for dying on her arse and she could get home and see whether they let Charlie out.

Jake went on first and his heart sank as he saw he was faced with a whole cohort of the working classes, many red-faced blokes on their way home from Saturday shiftwork who had stopped in for a

263

pint and were hoping for a lot of sexism, a touch of racism and plenty of filth served up for their delectation; Jake Ashkenazy was certainly not what they wanted.

'Hello brothers,' he began.

'I'm not your fucking brother, you cunt,' said one of the red-faced drinkers. 'I wouldn't have a brother who sounded like he'd been born with a silver spoon in his gob. Gonna tell us what's wrong with our lives and how you're gonna put it all right for us, are you?'

That was exactly what Jake had been intending to do. He wondered whether to persevere and desperately hoped a lot of knob jokes would come to mind. Unfortunately they didn't and after a brief struggle, Jake Ashkenazy was strangled at the birth of his act and resolved immediately to do a tour of arts centres in the hope that he would only encounter the middle classes who loved being told they were working class and wouldn't dream of aiming the 'C' word at him.

Jake slunk back into the dressing-room as the red-faced drinkers claimed their first victim. They had left Mal Fogarty well alone because they liked him and he was one of their own, but these posh wankers from London were a different matter.

Sarah had been a bemused spectator when all this was going on and felt sorry for Jake Ashkenazy because he was good-looking, although of the few minutes he actually had managed to perform before he left the stage, not a word had she understood. Mal Fogarty, on the other hand, she immediately warmed to because he reminded her of the men who had surrounded her mother while she was growing up. Her mother had been the only negative part of the equation, being grasping, spiteful and unfriendly to a series of men who loved her to distraction for her wild looks and quick humour, something that sadly, Sarah hadn't inherited.

She was just thinking what a pain in the arse her mother was when there was a tap on her shoulder.

'Long time no see, Sez! How you doing, gel?' followed by an unmistakable high-pitched laugh.

'Mum, It's great to see you,' said Sarah, wondering if it was.

'Well, I couldn't pass up the chance to see you and your big-nosed hippy friend, could I?' said Connie McBride. 'And hey presto, here you are. Besides, I quite fancy the MC.'

'Mum,' said Sarah wearily, 'he's married. Leave him alone, will you.'

'All's fair in love and war, Sez,' replied Connie sagely. 'Can I get you a drink, love? Anyway I'm bored shitless with Philip—he's getting right on my tits.'

Philip was Connie's longterm and longsuffering boyfriend, a mild-mannered, slightly hirsute bank manager in his early sixties who couldn't believe his luck when Connie had dragged him into her bed and done things he had never been allowed to even think about with his wife.

'How's that gorgeous Billy?' demanded Connie, who had heard about him from her daughter during one of their rare phone conversations. Sarah wasn't sure whether to tell her mother what had happened for fear she might jump on a train to South London and try to bed him, as she had always flirted relentlessly with any of Sarah's boyfriends whenever they had come down to see her.

Sarah asked her mother for a vodka and tonic and Connie went to the bit of the bar where Mal was standing and leaned against him as much as she could without becoming a surrogate Siamese twin. The landlord had called a bar break in between each act as he thought it would drive the normal punters mad if they had to wait until a proper interval. Connie had been in the pub for some time, apparently, and had managed to get herself quite pissed.

'When's your mate on?' she enquired genially, leaving Sarah to hope that when Flower came on, Connie wouldn't feel the need to converse with her.

'She's on now,' said Sarah, as Mal introduced Flower who had been shaking just behind the thin curtain that separated them, the stars, from the riff-raff.

Flower walked up to the microphone. 'Good evening,' she said. 'I was at the demo up in the City today. Hit a few crusties, caused a bit of mayhem.'

The audience looked bemused.

'Still,' said Flower, 'it's a great life being a fucking copper.'

Big laugh.

'Sarah never told me you was a copper,' came a voice from the front row where Connie had deposited herself to gaze adoringly upon the portly physique of Mal.

'Bloody hell,' said Flower, 'I didn't realise that Camilla Parker Bowles moonlighted as a stripper in Maidstone.'

There was a huge roar of laughter from the crowd. Flower felt exhilarated and really mean all

266

'What are we going to do about bloody Sarah?' said Flower.

'Don't we just have to let her get on with it?' said Martha.

'You've changed your tune,' said Flower. 'You were all for intervening a little while ago.'

'I know, I'm sorry,' said Martha. 'It all seemed so much more important when I was on my own but now to be honest I've got stuff to be getting on with.'

'Oh thanks,' said Flower. 'That makes me feel really good. So I'm the saddo without a life, am I?'

'I know it sounded like that,' said Martha, 'and I'm really sorry.'

'I'm sorry too. It's just that I've been feeling so irritable and scared lately. That weird heckler was there again last night and just as I felt on top of my game and ready to tackle him, he disappeared. But I'm worried he'll come round again and Charlie keeps not getting to the gigs and I'm frightened,' said Flower shakily.

'Just shoot the bastard,' said Martha cheerily. 'You've got a gun, Calamity Jane.' Flower put her finger to her lips. She didn't want Ted to know. He actually might suggest something sensible, like handing it in to the police.

'Anyway,' said Flower, 'enough of that now—are you coming to my big debut at the Comedy Store tonight?'

'Oh, I wish I could,' said Martha, 'but it's just not possible with John. I feel I can't leave him.'

Flower thought with such a straight name as John, the poor kid was really going to get bullied in a playground full of Feargals and Jacks.

'What about Junior's mum?' said Flower. 'Go

271

on, Martha, it's really important to me. I'm haemorrhaging support as it is.'

'I did think of her and asked actually, but she's going to be out,' said Martha. 'I'm really sorry but I wouldn't trust anyone else.'

'OK,' said Flower dejectedly. 'I don't suppose that Sarah will come either, now she's back with Billy.'

'Sorry,' said Martha. 'I know it means a lot to you. Perhaps we could bring John with us. I'm sure it'll be OK for one night.'

'Martha,' said Flower, 'there's nothing worse than a baby at a comedy gig. It's like a hypomanic at a funeral.'

'I don't really understand that reference,' said Martha, 'but that joke might come in handy if you're ever performing at the Royal College of Psychiatrists' summer ball.'

'That's my problem,' said Flower. 'Too intelligent for the masses.'

John, who had been dozing on Ted's lap, woke up and started to cry so Martha picked him up and began feeding him.

There was a sharp, unChristian knock on the door.

'I'll get it,' Flower offered.

It was the Rev Brian and Pat, Martha's sister Mary and her incredibly shrunken, bony husband Derek.

'Hello,' said Flower, 'come in.'

The quartet were ushered into the sitting room where Martha had very quickly roused Ted who was trying to smooth his hair, flatten his erection and sort out the drool that had dribbled down onto his shirt during the snooze.

'Christ, you pick your moments,' said Martha. 'Why don't you ever phone?'

'Because you'd tell us not to come,' said Pat.

Derek the skull sniggered and wheezed at this and wrinkled his nose as if there was an unpleasant smell in the flat. There was—John had just produced one.

'And what brings you up to this charming area?' said Martha. 'Bit of sightseeing round the estate or an attempted conversion on the teenage murder squad?'

'Don't be sarcastic, dear,' said the Rev Brian. 'You're a mother now and you have to grow up a bit.'

'Bollocks,' said Martha and her father shuddered as if he had been stabbed.

'Let's not get off on the wrong foot,' said Pat mildly.

'Sorry,' said Martha. 'All right, I'll put the kettle on. Here you are.' She handed John over to her mother.

'I'll come with you,' said Mary.

Mary and Martha had never liked each other much, but in the kitchen as Martha made a big tray of tea, things were surprisingly friendly and they found themselves having a laugh about their respective men.

'We could go to fancy dress with them as Laurel and Hardy,' said Martha and got a laugh out of Mary.

'Look,' said Mary, 'I know I haven't been much of a sister.'

'Stop right there,' said Martha. 'Let's not do the happy families thing quite yet.'

'Wait till I have mine,' said Mary, 'then we will.'

273

'God, you're not pregnant, are you?' said Martha.

Mary nodded. Martha gave her a hug.

'We wanted to tell you all together. Mum and Dad are staying for the weekend.'

Martha felt slightly overwhelmed by all this family closeness. 'Are you going back tonight?' she said.

'Well,' said Mary, 'we were thinking, me and Derek, about staying in a hotel.'

'I don't suppose . . .' said Martha. 'You see, there's something really important I have to do tonight but I wouldn't trust anyone to babysit but you. I'll only be gone a few hours.'

'Express some milk,' said Mary. 'I'll give it to him in a cup.'

Mary made it sound easy but Martha knew she faced three-quarters of an hour tethered to a sadistic bit of plastic pumping away with all the dignity of a regimented Jersey milker to produce two teaspoons of the bloody stuff.

Pat and Brian were chatting in the sitting room with Ted whose job they hadn't been told about yet and so were fondly imagining that this big ugly bear of a man did something reassuringly dull, like working for the council.

Martha decided that bridge could be crossed at a later date and then scolded herself for not immediately telling her father and getting some pleasure out of it.

Flower was pleased to see Martha's highly dysfunctional family all together in one place and getting on reasonably well for a change. She felt the weight of the show that evening hanging over her like a big black sponge preventing her from concentrating on anything else, from relaxing or from having a normal day in any form at all. Martha through all the fug of family and John recognised this and said to Flower, 'Why don't you just go home, have a really long hot bath, relax and take it easy before tonight.'

'Yes, I think I will,' said Flower and headed off. She switched her phone back on. There were three messages from Charlie apologising, which just got on her nerves.

The afternoon seemed to last a couple of days and by six o'clock Flower felt insane with nervous tension. She was also tired and had a headache—not the perfect condition, it has to be said, for doing your best gig.

She wondered whether she should medicate herself with something from Charlie's medicine box, a cornucopia of homoeopathic cures for anything you cared to name. Flower never took anything for anxiety but today felt that she needed a calming influence to cocoon her from the worst excesses of the show.

'Take the little yellow tablet,' said Charlie, 'in the smallest Russian doll in the medicine box,' for he had an odd, yet reasonably well organised system. 'I got that from some bloke last Saturday. He says it's a German homoeopathic cure for stress. That should do you.'

Flower located it and popped it in her mouth. It wasn't a homoeopathic cure for stress, but a very strong amphetamine that the joker had given to Charlie in the hope that he would take it and a comedy situation might develop. Within minutes her extremities started to burn.

Flower's mobile rang. It was Sarah.

'Hi,' she said. 'Your big night—can we come? I really want to support you but I can't very well tell Billy to stay at home.'

Great, thought Flower, her mind changing course unpredictably, more fucking stress. Why can't all the bastards stay at home and let me go and die a little death then forget about comedy and go back to my job.

Before leaving, she bathed and changed into something very neutral so she wouldn't have to consider if what she wore had any effect on the reaction she got.

The gun was in one of her bags, wrapped up in an innocuous-looking piece of material. Flower, who unwittingly was heading up the scale of arousal by the second, looked at it and put it in her pocket which already contained her set list. She then remembered she'd forgotten to put her lucky pants on, located them annoyingly in the washing basket after the Maidstone gig and sprayed them with a squirt of sandalwood in a gesture Martha would have been proud of, then slipped them on.

Charlie kept quiet and very much in the background. He knew the score before these shows: Flower could be really vicious when in a pre-performance paddy.

They arrived at the Comedy Store at eleven; the show was due to start at twelve. Flower managed to get Charlie, Martha and Ted, and Billy and Sarah in for free. She felt decidedly odd and said to Charlie, 'Are you sure that stuff that guy gave you is OK?'

'Of course,' said Charlie, whose network of mates/suppliers extended through squats up and down the country. 'It could be the four cans of

276

lager you had at home.'

'This is going to be awful,' said Flower, but in some ways because she was out of her head she felt quite elated and excited, as if that night was finally going to sort her out and show everyone she could do comedy.

The audience was also excited and some were quite pissed, while the old troupers who had done this gig many times sat dejectedly in the dressing-room . . . just another day at work for them. Flower's nervousness injected a sense of foreboding into them though.

The compère was Adrian Mole, his real name, a sweet-tempered rather bumbling Lincolnshire-born computer programmer whom everyone loved.

At one point Flower found herself alone in the dressing-room with Dick Knob. She hadn't seen him since that awful gig at the college which prompted her to go with him and get the gun.

Dick Knob always stormed it in the late show.

'Take the gun on as a joke,' he said, 'and wave it if someone heckles.'

'I haven't got it with me,' said Flower.

Dick Knob threw her a look which said, 'I don't believe you.'

The unreconstructed Australian comic Pat Denny was pacing up and down and wondering whether to try out a joke about Australian women looking like horses' arses. He felt safer in London but had been followed round half of Australia by a small coterie of feminist students who had made his life a misery by turning up at his gigs and shouting words like 'Rapist' at him, which didn't exactly improve his reception.

Jake Ashkenazy turned up, looking sheepish

after his diatribe to Flower about selling out the night before. Another comic had fallen by the wayside and he'd been offered a slot. He was lathering himself with false hope again.

Double act, The Fuckwits, were playing cards and drinking beers.

Adrian went on and tried to calm the audience down. That night it consisted of a few stag-night groups of City boys whose sole aim was to get alcohol down and up again as quickly as possible and were foolishly going to see a stripper after the comedy show, by which point their genitals would be in no fit state to respond. There were also lots of tourists who'd been in the West End all night and so were quite drunk, and many groups of friends from out of town on a special night out.

Flower was on last and had two hours to wait. She watched the progress of the other performers on the small monitor in the dressing-room.

Meanwhile, up at the bar Charlie, Billy, Sarah, Ted and Martha could not be said to be getting on like a house on fire. Ted and Billy were niggling at each other because Ted could somehow sense that Billy had some hold over Martha and resented this enormously. Martha had discovered the incredible elastic noose of motherhood was trying to catapult her back to the flat and John, but she kept telling herself to be strong and at least give Flower the support she deserved on her first big night. She too felt a sense of foreboding and wondered if Flower had the gun but was too scared to ask as she seemed jittery and unpredictable.

Martha looked from the handsome Billy to old horse-face Ted and was genuinely glad that she was with Ted. Also, of course, she was still relishing telling the Reverend Brian about the lap-dancing club and awaiting his reaction which she predicted would be nuclear, particularly if Ted was her husband by that point too.

Jake Ashkenazy's name was announced by Adrian the compère, who looked towards the door onto the stage, which stayed resolutely closed.

'Jake Ashkenazy!' he said again, rather desperately.

'Oh, the poor git's bottled it,' said Ted and the action of the comedy faded into the background as they started talking again.

Martha wondered whether she should phone Mary and Derek to see if John was all right. Ted advised against it—he was having too good a time. This was lucky as John had been screaming his head off since Ted and Martha left and had sprayed Derek's velour-look maroon jumper with a particularly pungent strain of baby vomit. He had refused the bottle and both Derek and Mary had separately felt that Mary's pregnancy might have been a very serious mistake.

Sarah and Charlie both seemed nervous and slightly jumpy for their own reasons. Billy looked pleased with himself though and was basking in the relief of Sarah having stayed with him, his resolve to change strengthened and his proposal of marriage just a couple of hours away from making the transition from thought to speech.

The stage-manager of the Comedy Store, after Jake Ashkenazy's untimely exit, had told all the acts to do a bit longer while he combed the audience for any comics who might agree to do Jake's slot.

Dick Knob stormed the show, of course.

Pat Denny started very mildly with some stuff about being an Australian in London and then moved to the heart of his act.

'Most girls in Australia look like horses' arses,' he said, to the delight of the stag-night groups who whooped and cheered and shouted, 'So do they here, mate!'

'Really?' said Pat, surprised to be getting such an easy ride. And then he got an even bigger surprise as a lump of horse manure hit him full in the face. This serendipitously appropriate faecal heckle was the work of a Central London women's group who had been phoned by the Australian students and purely by chance had planned to go to the Comedy Store on the day one member's dad had had a delivery of manure for his roses and just on the off-chance she'd popped some in her handbag.

Pat Denny couldn't come back from that and left. It was looking like a short show.

However, The Fuckwits could always be relied upon to save the day. Working on the premise that one in two people love jokes about snot and farting, they produced a tour de force of bodily effluence which the stag-night groups would remember for the rest of their lives.

Eventually, and she thought it would never happen, Flower's name was announced and she went on to a pissed, tired, but essentially cheerful crowd.

There was some immediate barracking which usually met the arrival of a woman onstage and extended through the continuum of their suitability as a sexual partner to some serious misogyny, which always came from at least five or so members of the audience. The one consolation was that they all shouted together so no individual piece of abuse could be heard, apart from a continuous stream of low-level heckling from a familiar voice in the front row. Flower could see nothing, nor could she bear to dip down beneath the spotlight and see exactly who her tormentor of the past few weeks had been. She thought the voice sounded a bit like Charlie's.

In a split second she elected to throw away her prepared material and in her amphetamine-befuddled brain decided she could just surf.

'How many of you blokes in the audience beat their partners?' she asked. There was a ripple of puzzled surprise and she added, 'And I don't mean at pool last week.'

People laughed as their tension eased slightly, even though the joke wasn't very good.

'My friend's boyfriend hits her,' said Flower, 'and sometimes she doesn't even deserve it because the dinner's quite nice. Fair enough if the gravy's lumpy, eh?'

Confusion was the main effect of this statement on the audience although the stag-night group continued to cheer.

'The funny thing is,' said Flower, 'we—that is, my friend Martha and I—thought the best way to deal with it might be to kill him.' The audience laughed cheerily and then laughed harder as Flower pulled out her gun.

'I know you think this is a replica,' she said, 'but look.' She pointed the gun at the ceiling and fired and some plaster exploded and crashed down. A low murmur heralded the beginnings of audience panic.

Flower realised that Billy, Ted, Martha, Sarah and Charlie were in front of her, looking

281

constipated facially, but their body language conveyed the message they might be incontinent at any time.

'Come on,' said Charlie, in the tones of a hostage negotiator. 'Give us the gun. You're off your face, love.'

'No, you get up here, Charlie,' said Flower, pointing the gun right at him. 'I want to talk to you . . . and the others too.' She motioned to Martha, Ted, Billy and Sarah to join Charlie and they shuffled up, hearts beating fast. The audience members couldn't quite make up their minds whether to rush out in a panic, screaming their heads off in case this disturbed hippy shot them, or stay and watch what was essentially the fascinating dénouement of a friendship crisis. Flower wasn't bothered either way. Her intention was to resolve her life, not keep an audience watching her only because of the threat of a bullet through the head. Consequently, the nervous ones dropped to their hands and knees and made their way quietly out of the door at the back, several of them choosing to phone newspapers and TV stations on the way and all of them forgetting that the police might be more appropriate.

Luckily, the manager of the club had walked to the office and called the police who began to put together an operation that would maybe have flushed out some IRA terrorists but was slightly over the top for a pissed-up hippy woman full of amphetamine.

'Right,' said Flower, her words being picked up by some floor microphones which were used for the improvisation show on a Wednesday night. 'Seeing as we're all here, we might as well sort out a few

282

things and then we can all go home and get on with our lives. *Comprende?'*

Charlie winced. Flower would never use a word like that if she was sober.

'Flower,' he started.

'Shut up!' shouted Flower. 'You're always . . .' she searched for the right word '. . . heckling me. In a nice way, sure, but it amounts to the same thing. I never get to say what I want. I don't want you to interfere. I need to sort this out my own way. Keep it shut, will you?'

Charlie nodded.

'Are you the one who keeps following me around heckling me?' said Flower, staring at him very hard and holding the gun surprisingly steadily for a person who had consumed a pillful of consciousness-altering chemicals.

'You're fucking joking, aren't you?' said Charlie. 'Surely—'

'Just say yes or no,' said Flower.

'No, of course not! You've got to trust me,' said Charlie.

'And do you trust me?' said Flower.

Charlie hesitated for a split second.

'You see!' shouted Flower. 'You don't, you never have and I know you're a nice bloke and all that, but you're driving me mad with your suspicion and twenty-four-hour surveillance. I can't relax.'

Charlie was wondering whether to make a grab for the gun. He couldn't believe that this mild-mannered, sweet woman had turned into a gun-toting tower of unpredictability. This was several big steps up from the kitten-kicking diva of PMT fame.

Perhaps Sim will make a story out of this one

283

day, he thought, and it will be a fuck of a sight more interesting than any of the bollocks he normally comes out with. It also occurred to him that one's thinking really clears in circumstances such as these.

Flower noticed someone in the front row had their hand up.

'Yes?' she said.

'Can I go to the toilet, please?' said the young man, a sweat breaking out as he tensely tried to avoid her eyes. Flower was shocked at the degree of deference he was demonstrating, even through the fog of her altered perception.

'Go on,' she said tersely, and he scuttled off as if he was under fire.

This awareness of her own power gave Flower the push she needed to turn the gun towards Billy. The audience gasped.

'Well?' she said.

'Well, what?' he answered nervously, having shrunk in stature, his usual cockiness missing.

'Let's hear from you about your behaviour over the last few months, shall we?'

The audience strained forward. They were almost enjoying themselves.

'Look, Flower,' said Billy, 'I know you and Martha hate my guts and I don't blame you. I realise I've been a right little shit all my life really and I've got away with it 'cause I always picked on people who were scared of me.'

'Go on,' said Flower.

'I can't,' said Billy. 'I don't know what else to say.'

'You can tell us why you've been hitting Sarah for a start,' said Flower.

284

'Yes,' murmured the audience: a surreal soap opera had sprung to life in front of their eyes.

'I don't know,' said Billy. 'She just gets on my tits sometimes. Women do.'

'Why, what do we do that's so irritating?' said Flower, enunciating every word slowly and sarcastically.

'Shall I be really honest?' said Billy.

'Yes,' said all the women in the room under their breath.

'You're all too vulnerable, smarmy and clinging sometimes . . . and like a dog I want to kick,' he said. 'Sometimes I can't stand the condition of being loved by a woman. It chokes me.'

This was the most insightful and possibly the most intelligent thing Billy had ever said in his life and it left him with a very surprised look on his face.

'All?' said Sarah and Martha together.

'Yup, pretty much, eventually,' said Billy, 'and I don't mean it in a bad way. It's just the way I feel.'

'So why are you like it?' said Sarah, throwing a glance across at Flower to check it was all right to take questions from the floor.

'I don't know,' said Billy. 'I was just brought up that way, I suppose, and I've never even thought about it.'

'Well, maybe you should if other people are getting it in the neck,' said Martha.

'I grew up with it,' said Billy wearily, as though he had told this story a hundred times before when in fact it was the first time.

He continued: 'I watched my father treat my mother like shit for all of my childhood and I suppose I just absorbed it. I didn't like the way my dad treated her and it made me angry, but look at me now—I'm almost a carbon copy of my old man. Perhaps it's unavoidable.'

Martha shuddered. Was she a carbon copy of the Rev Brian?

'And even when my mum was being treated really badly, I remember feeling guilty for thinking she was so pathetic. My dad had her in such a state that he just had to look at her in a certain way or make her jump by dropping something and she'd do what she was told. She started to have this expression on her face constantly as if she'd been hit, even when she hadn't, and I found it repulsive and wished she'd sort herself out.'

'Not your dad, then?' said Flower.

'Eh?' said Billy.

'Why should your mum have had to sort herself out?' said Flower. 'It was your dad who was the problem.'

'S'pose,' said Billy, hanging his head and looking like this initial foray into self-analysis had killed off half his brain cells, including the ones that controlled his neck muscles.

'You're a bully,' said Flower, 'and you rely on your physical strength to intimidate people. It's just not fucking fair.'

'I know,' said Billy. 'I'm not proud of it, you know.'

'Are you not?' said Martha, trying inappropriately to get a one-liner in. Everyone ignored her.

'It's partly my fault, you know,' said Sarah.

Flower cackled, a very high-pitched sound she had not heard herself emit before and it quite unsettled her. To Charlie it signified that she was

286

well on the way to being completely out of control.

'Oh, don't make me laugh,' said Flower. 'You're not going to do that old talking doormat "I deserved it" bollocks, are you, Sar?'

'Look, Flower, we're not all bloody lesbians, you know,' said Sarah.

'I presume that's your way of saying we're not all left-wing separatist feminists, is it?' said Flower.

'Maybe,' said Sarah, continuing, 'and we're not all going out with Harry the Fucking Hippy either. What I mean is that I have sat there and taken it over the months and surely that's given him' (she pointed at Billy as if he was a road sign) 'the message that it's all right. I should've left ages ago, but I stupidly thought if he really liked me he wouldn't hit me.'

'Fair enough assumption,' said Ted, who had been quiet up until this point.

'Look, Flower,' said Charlie, 'I'm not being annoying, but I suggest we wrap this up fairly soon because some of these punters must've told the Old Bill you're on one in here. Surely it's only a matter of time before they send a sniper in.'

This had the opposite effect from what Charlie intended. Flower, losing what composure she had left, screamed at Charlie to shut up with such a degree of vehemence that the audience became rather frightened and all looked at the floor lest they incur Flower's wrath.

'Look, I just want to sort Billy out and find out who heckled me,' said Flower, 'then we can all go home.'

'Billy doesn't need you to sort him out,' said Sarah. 'He'll do it himself.'

'Well, he hasn't looked much like doing that so

287

far,' said Flower.

'Come on, you two, don't fall out,' said Martha. 'Us girls have got to stick together.'

'What, even when you've fucked my boyfriend?' said Sarah.

Ears pricked again in the audience, bowels loosened inside Martha. She was too shocked to construct an argument against this statement so just looked sheepishly at the ground and said, 'How did you know?'

' 'Cause it was bloody obvious,' said Sarah. 'What else could have happened? You look guilty as hell every time I see you and you talk rubbish every time we mention that night.'

'So why didn't you come round and slap me about a bit?' said Martha, realising as the words came out of her mouth that this wasn't the most tactful thing to say, given the circumstances.

'Because,' said Sarah, 'I suppose I was hoping that if I just ignored it, it would all go away and that Bill and I could get back on an even keel again and that we would never need to bring it up.'

'So why have you?' said Martha.

' 'Cause I'm bloody livid,' said Sarah.

'Me too,' said Ted.

'Excuse me,' said Flower, waving the gun about as if it was a wilting bunch of flowers, 'but I think you'll all find this is my fucking crisis and I'm in charge. Now let's sort the heckler business out. Was it you, Billy?' She turned the gun back to him.

'No, I swear on my mother's grave it wasn't,' said Billy.

'Fucking drama queen,' mumbled Ted under his breath, having developed a recent desire to punch Billy in the face.

288

Sarah added, 'I thought you could only say that if your mother was actually dead.'

'I believe you, Billy,' said Flower.

'Perhaps it's a stranger, and he's gone home and you'll never find out,' said Ted.

'Shit,' said Flower. 'That kid that just went to the toilet—do you think—?'

'No,' said Charlie. 'Couldn't be.'

'Are you *sure* it's not you, Charlie?' said Flower.

'Oh, for Christ's sake,' said Charlie, 'why would I, someone who loves you to bits, follow you round heckling you? We're not all like Billy, you know.'

'That was below the belt,' said Billy.

'So hit me then,' said Charlie. 'Everyone else does.'

For once a fist did not visit Charlie's face, nor a boot his bollocks. This caused him to launch into a speech he had been planning to make for some time, and now seemed a perfect opportunity.

'Look, Flower,' he said, 'I can't tell you how hard it's been to see you dragging yourself round this godforsaken comedy circuit trying to get laughs, not to mention finding that bloody heckler. In fact, I know you'll be angry, but one night I did come to see you and heard the guy. I tried to get across the audience to see who it was but by the time I'd got there, I couldn't find him. Please stop putting yourself through this, will you? You're too nice for all this. It's more Martha's sort of thing.'

'Oh cheers,' said Martha.

'Give up and come home. I'll really make an effort not to be so possessive and all that shit, I promise,' continued Charlie.

A tear rolled down Flower's face. She knew Charlie was right and that she wasn't any good. In

289

fact, on the rare occasions Martha had been to a club she'd always come out with far funnier things from her seat in the audience.

'Come on, Flower, give us the gun,' said Charlie. 'Let's go.'

Flower drooped. She lowered the gun and began to walk towards Charlie. The dressing-room door opened and Dick Knob, who had been watching the whole thing on the CCTV in there, sauntered past.

'Great piece of entertainment,' he said. 'Right beautiful.'

A massive firework went off in Flower's memory as neurones began firing to tell her that the word 'beautiful' held the clue to the identity of the heckler.

'Fuck me, it was you!' she shouted, wheeling round to face Dick Knob and retaining the steadiness of hand that had surprisingly characterised her gun-use all evening.

'Me what, Princess?' he said, feigning casual.

'You who's been heckling me,' said Flower.

'Nah, you've got the wrong geezer, Flower. I'd never do that to you,' said Dick. 'I love you. Don't you know that? Oh shit, what am I saying? I know the heckling was a fucking weird thing to do but I didn't want you to leave the circuit and I thought you were about to, so I was doing my best to harden you up, to give you that extra shell you need to cope. Christ, if you think you've had it bad so far, just wait till your career progresses and the critics start on you. They're far worse than any pissed-up old cunt in the audience, I'm telling you. No one survives them, even the ones who seem the hardest. That hairy wanker's right, you are too

290

nice. So I was just trying to prepare you for the sort of shit you're bound to get if you stay around in this job because fuck it, Flower sweetheart, you're bloody gorgeous and I adore you. Shoot me now if you want.'

Dick started to get a hard-on at the very thought of being shot down on the stage of the Comedy Store by the woman he loved.

Even though he looked so greasily forensic Martha found herself slightly jealous at this disturbed declaration of love and looked towards Ted for one to equal it. Unfortunately Ted was still coping with the idea of Billy entering her flat that night . . . and her, of course. Charlie had a fist raised.

'Calm down, Charlie,' said Flower. 'There's no need for that. He loves me—you don't have to hit him for that.'

'Do you love him?' said Charlie.

'Of course not,' said Flower and then, seeing how crestfallen Dick looked, wished she'd left out the 'of course'.

'Is it 'cause I'm ugly?' said Dick.

'You're not ugly,' said Flower.

'Oh yes he is!' tried a few wags in the audience.

'Don't listen to them,' said Flower.

'Bollocks,' said Ted, who'd barely said a word all night. ' 'Course he's plug ugly and so am I, and it's something you have to learn to live with. Not for me the romantic gesture coupled with a granite jaw and steely good looks framed with wild black curly hair. Oh no, just an overweight victim of acne whose limbs appear to have been designed for someone three times my age and whose hair has the texture of greasy spaghetti. I've been laughed

291

at, spat on, sneered at, avoided, put down, ignored, kicked, beaten up, used as a trampoline and left on the pavement in a very ugly heap so many times I've lost count, but I've had to put up with it.'

'What about surgery?' said Sarah, the queen of tactful interjection.

Martha drew in a sharp breath at this innocently cruel remark, but Ted just laughed.

'Christ no,' he said. 'I just went into a job that suited my face. Everyone expects me to be a pervert, so why disappoint them? Confound them from inside the job, that's what I plan to do. I run my club well, I'm kind and I pay good money. And it's as a result of that club that I've met the most disturbed, unpredictable, silly, petty, messy, stubborn, most gorgeous woman in the world, we've got a son and that's me sorted. You'll just have to keep looking, Dick old son.'

'Yeh,' said Dick, still reeling from the response of Flower to his secret, the one he had nursed for two years. He couldn't believe his chance of happiness had been trashed so decisively and so quickly.

Martha beamed a broad grin. 'I always wanted an ugly one,' she said, 'so no one would try and nick him off me and I've hit the bloody jackpot with Ted.' Ted started to laugh.

Martha continued, 'Reluctant as I am to join amateur psychology hour, Flower and I just wanted Billy to stop hitting Sarah, whether they sorted things out with each other or not. Sarah and Ted, I am so sorry I ended up sleeping with Billy. I'm not going to come up with any excuses but my raging hormones and drink contributed. It will never happen again and I'm sorry if I've hurt anyone. In a

292

weird way I suppose I thought Sarah might leave Billy if he was unfaithful and that would sort the situation out.'

'Did you really think that?' said Ted.

'No,' said Martha, 'but I refuse to accept I am quite such a moral bankrupt.'

'I'm not sure I can forgive you,' said Sarah.

'Oh dear,' said Martha.

'But I'll have a good go,' said Sarah.

'Fucking great,' said Dick Knob, 'so everyone's happy except me, then?'

They all nodded solemnly and the audience clapped.

Dick Knob strolled dejectedly past the audience and up the stairs.

'Hang on,' said Martha. 'Flower, didn't we say the only way to absolutely guarantee that Billy is sorted out is to threaten to shoot his testicles off if he ever touches Sarah again?'

Billy instinctively covered his bollocks, having found it difficult to decide whether Martha was joking or not.

'Yes, it's a joke,' she said.

Dick Knob appeared again, at the back of the room.

'There's fucking loads of police out there,' he screamed.

'Well, I suggest,' said Flower, picking up the microphone out of its stand, 'that you, the audience, file out in an orderly fashion with your hands up and we'll all come out at the end and explain ourselves. But hang on one little minute, I haven't finished my set yet. Down you all sit.'

'Flower,' said Charlie, exasperated.

'Well, fuck it,' said Flower, 'I haven't shot

anyone. At least let me do a couple of jokes. And they are the last ones I'll ever do.'

A beleaguered police Inspector with a loudhailer and two vanloads of policepersons who could shoot in a straight line shook his head and turned in a puzzled fashion to his colleague.

'They're all killing themselves laughing down there now,' he said.

'As long as they're not killing each other with that gun,' replied his colleague.

'You should be a fucking comedian,' replied the Inspector.